# WHAT KARLA WANTS

New school, new friends, hot football captain and an invite to a Friday night party could spell disaster. Karla trusts anyone who will befriend her. This is just the way she is. But should she really be so trustful?

Karla moves from her rural childhood home to the bustling city unwillingly when her parents lose their home to foreclosure. She makes new friends almost immediately. After they invite her to a party so she can go out on a date with the football captain, she convinces her parents to let her sleep over her newly made friend's house, Carol. Maybe she is a bit too trusting of these new friends of hers. She begins to have second thoughts about going to this party at the last minute. Maybe she shouldn't have been so trusting?

# What Karla Wants

Linda Nelson

New Ipswich, NH United States

Keelaa B Publishing

http://lindajnelson.com

# ACKNOWLEDGMENTS

I would like to take the time to thank the Phoenix House Drug Rehab. If it had not been for the past times my son spent in their program, this book would never have been written. Particularly the adolescent program he was in during the year 2005.

The time he spent there not only was life altering for him but for me also.

# DEDICATION

This book is dedicated

To my son Chris and my daughter Megan

Thank you for teaching me to take a step back and to look at my own hopes and dreams.

May this book inspire both of you to follow your own dreams and passions.

In addition, I would like to give a special thank you to my love Mike for putting up with me while I rambled on about publishing this book,

Moreover, thank you to my Mom for believing in me.

# 1

"WE WOULDN'T HAVE TO DO THIS IF YOU'D GONE OUT AND GOTTEN a job as I asked you to."

"I looked for a job. I went out twice a week filling out job applications. Don't make this out to be about me," Mrs. Centon argued.

"Well, it is about you. Had you spent less money on booze and more on the bills, this would never have happened," Mr. Centon replied.

If you were a bird sitting on the branch next to the bedroom window, you would've heard the whole argument. However, just like Karla, you didn't hear the entire conversation. She only overheard the part about spending less money on booze and nothing about her mom needing to go out and find a job. As far as she knew, only her dad was the one who needed the new job. He'd been out of work for about three months before finding the one in Brantwood.

Looking out the bedroom window, you would've seen the street pocketed with potholes. It passed right in front of the house, giving the home a small front yard. A grove of pine trees clustered the front right side of the ranch style home.

If you wandered around in the yard, you would've smelled the freshly cut grass which covered the ground in the yard, waiting to be raked. More trees led around the boundary of the three-quarter-acre lot stopping on the other side of the house where the small driveway began.

Taken a walk up the rural street and you would've seen how it lined with similar homes mirroring each other up and down the street. About ten homes made up the housing development. Each house sat close to each other, all with large back yards.

A for-sale sign slowly swung back and forth in the yard close to the road. The sign beckoned passer-by with its sold sign hanging below the real estate name. Time showed its passing on the sign with the dents, chipped paint, and its rusted sides. It had seen better days.

A stiff breeze cut the sticky humid air from the west. It was one last hot day before the end of the summer. Labor Day weekend had begun with school starting on the coming Wednesday, and Karla would be missing the first few days of school. She needed to help her parents with the packing and moving. Her dad had already taken care of transferring her into the new school.

Karla didn't understand why all the rushing. Nevertheless, her mom had always been this way. Rush – rush – rush – that was her way of doing things. The only thing Karla could think of to explain why her mom always rushed about everything was so she would've plenty of time left to have that drink.

She hated it when her mom was drinking, which was almost every day. She was sure her dad was not happy with her drinking either. He just never seemed to make a big deal about it, at least not in front of Karla. But then again there were times he seemed never to be home. Before he lost his job, he was always working long hours. He said they needed the money. Karla was sure it was to avoid being home, so he wouldn't have to deal with her mom's drinking problem.

Karla frowned as she packed another box and began to think about her friends Sarah and Jody.

She'd been in the same school with the same classmates ever since first grade. Now that she was in tenth grade she was entering a different school system for the first time in her life.

Karla felt uneasy about moving and attending a new school. She was not terribly popular in this school, and she was afraid she wouldn't fit in the new school, either. "But then again maybe," she pondered.

Karla downright hated moving away from her friends, Sarah, and Jody. The three of them would hang out in her back yard under the old chestnut tree. Her dad had hung a tire swing from the sturdy branch when she was five. That same tire swing was still there with lots of knots in the rope it hung from. She'd to add another knot every time she grew another foot.

Sometimes she and her friends would even take off and go hang out down the street at the pond. It had a small sandy beach they sometimes went to wade in its water along the shore to cool off on a hot summer day. After hearing the pond had bloodsuckers, they didn't dare go out any further than their waists.

She was tired of packing and simply needed to talk to her friend Jan.

Karla peered out her bedroom window waiting for her friend to return home. She watched the driveways, which twined each other side by side with a small patch of grass separating them from each other.

A little red Honda pulled into Jan's driveway.

The tall driver slowly stepped out of the car and walked to the rear, opening the hatchback to remove several items from the car. She left the hatch open and made her way to her steps leading to the side door into her home.

Karla looked away from the window feeling glum about her task. She had a mess in her room. Empty boxes littered the floor of Karla's bedroom. She pushed them aside with a kick of her foot, sending a bunch of boxes sliding across the wooden floorboards. She opened her bedroom door, stepped out into the short hallway, and closed the door behind her. She passed a stack of unmade boxes, stacked against the wall.

Her parents' bedroom was at the very end of the hallway. The bathroom was across from her bedroom. In the other direction, the entrance led into the kitchen with the small dining room off to the right. Light flooded into the dining room and kitchen from the sliding glass patio door leading out to the little back porch.

Karla quickly passed through the kitchen with its piles of packed boxes. The living room looked bare. The pictures that'd hung on the walls all packed, leaving shadows where the pictures once hung.

She burst out the screen door letting it slam shut behind her with a bang. Grabbing the short railing, she made her way down the concrete steps and ran to greet the older woman, Jan.

Mrs. Centon yelled at Karla from the open screen door. "Karla, get back in here. I know you're not done packing, and we've to be done by Monday, and Sunday is the cookout. This all needs to get done… now."

"Yeah… Mom," Karla yelled back over her shoulder. "I'll be just a few minutes. I've to talk to Jan for a bit. I'll be right back."

She glared back at her mom. She didn't understand why her mom wouldn't let her have a break she was tired of packing.

"Make it quick then," Mrs. Centon shouted and retreated into the house.

Karla had planned to ignore her anyway.

The thirty-year-old woman had lived next to the Centons' for quite some time. She'd been Karla's babysitter when she was a toddler. Later on, she grew into a close family friend

Whenever Karla needed to talk to someone about things, things that kids don't want to talk to their parents about, she'd always go to Jan.

Like that first boy in elementary school, she'd liked. She was afraid her mother would pick on her about having a crush on a boy in her class. Therefore, she went to Jan about it. Karla always trusted Jan's opinions without fear of any adverse criticism.

The blonde haired woman walked down her steps with empty hands to retrieve the last batch of parcels from the hatch of her car. A smile formed on her face as soon as she saw Karla.

"Hi, Jan…"

She found Jan's smile infectious and smiled herself for the first time that day.

"Are you ready for the big move?"

"No."

Karla's smile quickly turned back into a frown. She'd been going around pouting ever since her parents had broken the news of the move to her about a month ago. At first, she thought they'd been playing some sort of joke on her by saying it. Then when the for-sale sign appeared on their front lawn, she knew it was for real.

Karla angrily kicked the ground with her foot, sending a stone skidding across the lawn.

"Jan, I can't take it. Why do my folks have to move? Don't they even care about me? Why don't they ask me what I want? Couldn't they just buy a house here in town?"

Karla looked up saw a strange look in Jan's hazel eyes.

She didn't want to leave her friends behind, and it seemed like no one actually understood or cared about her feelings. Karla wondered why things couldn't continue the way they were. She hated the world because of it and was pissed off.

"Your dad has a new job, and your folks found this great house," Jan said, concern resounding in her voice. "You'll be able to take part in classes or clubs that aren't even offered here at Medham High. Your dad's career change and this move are in your best interest."

Turning away to shield from view the tears forming in her eyes, Karla bitterly kicked another rock. She watched it bounce across the lawn and thought about how she was never going to see her friends ever again. She knew she was going to hate her folks for the rest of their lives for making her move away from her friends.

"But I don't want to move. What about my friends?"

Karla wiped the tears from the corner of her eyes with the back of her hand. She knew Jan could see her crying like a big baby. Moreover, she felt like one too but just couldn't help it. Her eyes just kept watering up every time she remembered her memories of her and her friends.

Karla flinched when Jan reached out to comfort her. She was herself pulled into Jan's comforting arms. After giving in, she began sobbing. All she wished was that Jan had been her mother. If she'd been her mom, then, she wouldn't have had to move away from her friends. Jan understood her better than her folks.

Finally, she found her composure and pulled away, standing on her own. She focused on the house, watching her bedroom curtain waving from the breeze. Karla detected a hint of barbecue chicken and fresh cut grass drifting from the neighborhood. Those were two of her favorite smells of summer.

"You're only moving a few towns away, I'm sure they'll keep in touch." Karla heard the frustration in Jan's voice. "You can call each other, and write. There is also the Internet, and your folks most likely will allow you've sleepovers with them."

Her mom was always letting her know how her friends weren't perfect enough for her to hang out with. "That I doubt. Mom never lets me have friends sleep over. She never lets me do anything," Karla replied.

She thought about how mean her mom tended to be toward her friends. They seemed to annoy her, but even Karla annoyed her at times. Thinking about this only made her feel worse.

"That can't be true. What about that time you told me she allowed Mindy to sleep over?" Jan said in disbelief.

"Yeah… That was way back when I was seven. She hasn't let me have anyone over since then," Karla muttered.

"Why not," Jan asked.

"Mindy got scared that night and woke up screaming. Then come morning, Mom was so mad when she found out Mindy had wet the bed." She leaned with Jan against her car and watched Little Amy ride her bike by, waving at her. Karla couldn't believe that it was her first time without training wheels. She was going to miss babysitting that kid.

"Have you ever asked her if you could've anyone else over since then?"

"No. I never dared to. She was so angry that night. I've been reluctant to ask her ever since."

"If you want, I can talk to her for you, maybe suggest you having a sleepover or two, just to help you with your transition into your new school," Jan said confidently.

"Would you do that for me? I'm afraid to ask her."

Karla perked up with a glimmer of hope. Maybe just maybe her folks would listen to Jan. She caught a glimpse of a blue jay flying into the tree in front of the house and watched it walk along the branch toward the bird feeder. Bobbing its head up and down, it hopped off the branch to land on the feeder. After a brief moment, it flew away.

"I'll talk to her on Sunday, during the cookout," Jan said, attempting to change the subject just a little bit. "I hear the new house you're moving into has an in-ground pool."

Karla still couldn't believe this about the house they were moving to. "That's what my folks say. I got to see it before I'll believe it."

Her parents seemed so excited about the new house. Karla was so frustrated by the fact they wouldn't let her in on where they were moving to, or what the place was like. They kept saying to her, "you're really going to like it."

"I got to get going; I've some errands I need to get done." Jan leaned forward, moving away from the car. "I'll talk to her tomorrow." She swatted at a mosquito as it buzzed around her head.

" Kay… and thanks…I'm going to miss you."

She gave Jan a goodbye hug. "Karla, I'll still be by for visits." She hugged Karla back. "Just because my favorite neighbor is moving away, it doesn't mean I won't still be close friends with you and your family. I've known you since you were just a little squirt just out of diapers. I'll miss you too, but I'll be by for visits. I promise."

"I've got to go and finish packing anyway before Mom yells at me again, see you tomorrow." Karla waved goodbye. She turned to face her house and made her way to the driveway. Then she crossed the connecting lawns.

"Bye," Jan called after Karla, causing her to stop and turn around.

Karla waved one last time and made her way back to her house. Finally, she had a small glimmer of hope. Maybe, Karla told herself, just maybe Jan would be able to convince her folks into letting her have her friends over for a sleepover.

She stopped at the screen door and surveyed the front yard one last time. Her eyes rested on the sold sign, reminding her of what was to come, making her upset once again.

Karla returned to her bedroom and began solemnly packing up all her things.

# 2

KARLA FINISHED PACKING ANOTHER BOX. SHE LIFTED IT UP AND stacked it on top of the pile that lined her bedroom wall. This pile of boxes now threatened to block her door to her closet. She left the closet door open for this very reason.

Empty hangers hung across the bar inside it. Stacks of ratty magazines still piled on its floor. A blanket rolled into a ball on the floor next to the magazines.

Karla reached for another box and began packing the magazines. She then heard her mother call her from the kitchen.

"Karla. Can you come help me?"

"Coming," she answered as she stood up from her kneeling position.

Her mother was in the kitchen preparing the cold-cuts, veggie and sandwich platters for their cookout today. They were expecting some of the neighbors and other families from the surrounding town. People they'd known for years. This was to be a good-bye cook out. Her parents had been planning it for several weeks, for Sunday, the day after signing the papers on their new home.

Her dad had griped about the money her mom was spending on this cookout. He said it was needless, and most of these people never actually spoke to them. He couldn't understand why she needed to hold a farewell party. This was beside the fact that they just downright couldn't afford to have a cook out anyway.

They'd argued well into the night, and of course, her mom had won out, only because her mom had already sent out the invitations with her dad's approval.

Karla was so-so about the cook out today. She actually liked having cookouts, but she didn't like saying goodbye to any of her friends. It was not as if she'd many friends, but just the same. Sarah and Jody weren't just any old friends. They were her best friends. She'd known them forever.

"Can you take this and put it on the table over next to the grill?"

Karla nodded.

Mrs. Centon held out the veggie platter for Karla to carry.

"Daddy will know which table he wants it on."

Her mom opened the sliding door for her.

"Just take it to him. Thanks, dear."

She carried the tray carefully down the steep steps of the back porch into the slightly sloping back yard.

Her dad was setting up the grill toward the far back yard where the grass met the tree line. A folding banquet table was set up off to the side of the grill while another table lay folded up against the side of the tool shed.

The tool shed was wide open exposing the items inside. The lawn mower moved and parked off to the other side of the shed, out-of-the-way for now. Lawn chair hung from a couple of the shed rafters. Rakes and shovels hung on the inside wall.

Karla stepped off the bottom step and onto the grass. Her flip-flops slapped at her heels. The thongs dug into her feet while walking down the slope.

She held out the tray to her Dad when she stepped up beside him.

"Where do you want this?"

He pointed to the table.

"Just put it over there."

Karla set the tray on the table next to the paper plates.

"Dad can I help you?"

Mr. Centon poured a bag charcoal into the grill.

"I'm all set. You need to help your mother."

He looked up and saw her frown.

"If you'd please.... For just this once will you help your mother without an attitude?"

Karla rolled her eyes, "Yeah, Dad."

She clenched her teeth on her way back to the porch. Her mother waited outside the door holding the next platter for her to bring to the table. She made about five trips back and forth to the table, bringing all the trays and plates of food her mother had prepared. She set the last dish on the table when the guests began to arrive.

Jan was the first one there. She was carrying a bowl of ambrosia. Her hair was done up in a neat bun, wisps of hair had fallen out on the sides framing her face. Karla smiled noting her khaki walking shorts and blue striped polo shirt weren't the best of her fashion statements. She was happy to see her anyway.

Mr. Centon then put Karla to the task of placing folding chairs all about the backyard. She was sorry she asked him earlier if he needed help. As soon as he'd seen her done with bringing the food to the tables had given her another job to do.

She'd to finish putting the chairs out before she could go over to see Jan.

She was frustrated by the hassle of setting up for the cookout. She wondered if people would bring their own chairs and all her work would be for nothing. Better yet, no one would sit down. They all would stand in groups just like the kids do in high school.

Karla gave her dad a glare and made faces at him while his back was turned.

Then, she'd look over her shoulder to see where Jan sat, talking with some of the other guests.

Finally, after what seemed like an hour later to Karla, even though it was only ten minutes later, she set out the last folding chair. The crowd was beginning to grow, and the people were starting to gather, moving into groups. As Karla suspected, some stood. She shot her dad another glare while he looked away.

Karla grumbled, "Dad I'm done. Can I see my friends now?"

Mr. Centon dismissed Karla with a quick wave. She wasted no time, afraid he'd find something else for her to do. Spotting the bowl of ambrosia on the table, she helped herself to a small bowl of it and found a spot away from the table under the old chestnut tree in the back yard. She started to make her way over to it, but then she spotted Jan.

Jan sat in one of the folding chairs Karla had set up, sitting with two other women. They'd left to go to the table for a plate of food. Karla took this opportunity to visit with her friend.

She took the seat next to Jan.

"Jan, this ambrosia is excellent," Karla said.

She stuffed another small spoonful into her mouth, eating it slowly to savor the taste.

"Can I get the recipe from you before I move?"

She was trying to feel better about relocating to a new town while hoping, really, really hoping, Jan would talk to her parents about letting her have a sleepover.

"Karla, I'm glad you like it. I'll give it to you only if you give me the recipe for those pickles you made," Jan smiled.

"Oh, those pickles are easy. Just take Dill pickles, coat the dried beef with cream cheese and wrap them around the pickles. Chill them for a couple of hours, and then slice them. That's how easy they're to make." She returned Jan's infectious smile.

"All right, but I've to write mine down, 'cuss I can't remember the recipe right off the top of my head like that," Jan snickered.

"Ha. Maybe I should write the pickle recipe down for you, in case you can't remember my three essential ingredients," she teased Jan over her forgetfulness.

"You're a Brat..." She paused for a moment in deep thought, "Maybe you'd better write it down for me. I'm not getting any younger. I forget things all the time. Not just recipes."

"Haha, you know I was just kidding," Karla laughed. "But I'll write it down anyway." She decided to change the subject. "Speaking of forgetting, did you remember to ask my mom about letting me have that sleepover?"

"Yeah, I did ask. She thinks sleepovers are a fantastic idea. She said she's surprised you haven't requested to have any since you were in first grade. She thought you didn't like sleepovers."

Jan took a bite of her hot dog.

Karla smiled. This was the best news she'd heard all week.

"I'll ask her the first week we move in. She better let me have one, or I'm moving in with you."

Karla noted the two women were on their way back to their chairs with full plates, and she graciously allowed Franny to take her seat back and sat on the ground in front of Jan, cross-legged.

"Relax. I'm sure she'll let you've your friends over," she reassured Karla. "Maybe even some pool parties." Jan grinned, "I hope someone remembers to invite me over to go in their pool with them."

Franny and Paula smiled too. They were quietly listening in on the conversation. Karla saw from the look on their faces, they also hoped for an invitation to the pool party.

This made Karla feel uncomfortable. She rocked up onto her knees.

She wondered if her parents showed the property to Jan. Karla asked, "How big is the pool?"

"I don't know. I'm sure it is decent sized. Oh, look. Here comes Sarah. I'm so glad to see you," Jan greeted Sarah, "Is Jody coming by?"

Sarah had tried to sneak up behind Karla. She was about to put her hands over Karla's eyes, but Franny's smile and the movement of her eyes gave away the surprise. Karla turned around just in time to avoid Sara's hands.

Karla couldn't help but notice Sara's bright green t-shirt with a giant yellow smiley face looking down at her. Sarah was always wearing some sort of bright colored shirt with her skinny jeans.

She could never figure out how Sarah was able to get into those jeans anyway. She'd tried them on once since Sarah and she were the same size, and no matter what she tried, she couldn't get them over her hips.

Karla stood up and brushed off her legs. "Um... I'll get that recipe from you later, Jan. We're just going to go..." She looked toward the chestnut tree.

Jan nodded, "yeah... You girls go chat. I'll see yah later with that recipe."

With the empty bowl in her hand, Karla led Sarah over to the chestnut tree. They passed a trash bucket on the way, and she pitched the bowl into it. She wondered where Jody was.

Sarah stopped and picked up a hot dog and soda on their way over to the tree. "So, Karla, your folks are really going to do it?" Sarah asked. "You're moving – Damn. Who are we supposed to hang out with over at the pond?" She took a bite of her hot dog. "Oh, and Jody got the job at the market, so she can't come by today," Sarah added.

Karla had taken soda from the cooler near the table. She cracked the tab on it and waited for the bubbles to settle. She then placed the can against her skin, feeling its cold side on her forehead. It was getting to be as hot today as it was yesterday. Maybe even hotter, Karla thought.

The shade of the chestnut tree beckoned them. Sarah followed Karla over to the tree, her dark brown ponytail sitting high on the back of her head, bounced up and down with her gaiety step. They sat down on the ground together, facing each other.

Karla set her soda down on the ground before her and plucked a blade of grass. "I can't believe this, either, Sarah. My folks didn't even discuss this move with me. It's as if they don't care about what I think or what I want. I don't wish to change schools."

Placing the blade of grass between her thumbs, she blew, making the blade buzz. Karla was sullen about moving. She wondered why they even had to move.

Sarah snapped up a little daisy from its base. She began twirling it between her fingers, fixing her hazel eyes on the flower head, looking deep in thought. "It'll be so boring around here without you," she finally said.

"I'm planning on asking my mom if I can have sleepovers after we get moved in." Karla discarded the grass blade and plucked up a buttercup, and removed the petals one by one, then tossed the mangled flower onto the ground.

"How far away are you moving?" Sarah asked while leaning back. She propped herself up with her arms extended on each side. Her ponytail almost touched the ground.

"We're moving to Brantwood, or so they say. I don't understand why Dad just can't travel to work as most people do. This rots... I've to pack my things, change schools, and then unpack everything. I'll never find any of my stuff."

Karla brushed the grass from the palms of her hands.

"I need another soda, want one?"

Karla stood and waited for Sarah to follow.

"Yup, I'll grab another one."

Some of the guests had moved their chairs closer toward the line of pine trees. They were apparently trying to avoid the heat of the afternoon sun. Karla saw her mom and dad mingling among the guest.

Sarah asked, "Did I hear Jan right, you guys will have a pool?"

"Yeah, so my folks say. I haven't seen it yet. I haven't even seen the house yet... it is as if it is some kind of secret or something. They never talk to me about any of it. If this doesn't work out, I'm skipping out. I'll move back here and live with Jan."

"Would Jan let you do that?" Sarah asked. "Wouldn't your parents be pissed if you did that?"

Karla tossed her can in the trash as Sarah handed her another one from the cooler. The cooler was getting low. She flipped up the lid to one of the other coolers sitting under the table. They grinned at each other over their discovery. The cooler had beer in it.

"I don't think mom would notice me missing." Karla motioned to the cooler full of beer.

"But I'm sure your dad would miss you," Sarah stressed. "Oh now that does look tempting, doesn't it," she smiled.

They laughed at the thought, but Karla didn't dare. Her mom probably would kill her. Giggling they went back to sit under the tree.

"Well, it can't be that bad that the town is pretty big. It's got a movie theater, bowling alley, and best of all a mall."

"Yeah, I know."

"And, you got a pool – how far are you from the school? Can you walk to the mall?" Sarah took a swig of her soda.

"Yeah, I can walk to school, and to the mall though I doubt Mom will ever let me hang out at the mall. She says that's how kids get into trouble."

"Well, when Jody and I sleep over, we'll ask her if we can all go to the movies and hang out at the mall. I'll get my mom to talk to her for you."

Karla looked in the direction of where she'd last seen her mom. She was now standing with a group of adult family friends.

She scoffed, "You know she'll say, NO, you know."

Sarah quickly changed the subject. "Your school must be enormous compared to ours. Did you pick your classes yet?"

"I'm going Tuesday to pick my classes and see the school. I hear the school is like, triple the size of Medham High."

"Hey, take your camera with you or better yet, send me a picture message when you check out your school."

"Why, did you get a cell phone?"

"Yup, I got it for my birthday," Sarah pulled her cell phone from her back pant pocket.

"Oh, cool. Let me see it," Karla said. She took the cell phone and opened it, checking the phone functions.

"Now I've to ask my folks for one. They should be able to afford one now. And they owe me since they're making me go and leave you guys behind.

I've to show Mom," Karla took the cell phone to her mom, with Sarah in tow.

The guests had begun to leave a little at a time. She noticed that Franny and Paula were no longer to be seen. She wondered what time it was getting to be.

"Mom... Check out Sara's new cell phone, she got for her birthday," Karla held the phone out for her mom to see, "Can I've one too?"

"We'll have to talk it over with your dad later," Mrs. Centon quickly glanced at the phone and then turned back to her current conversation.

Karla clenched her teeth. That always hurt her when her mother didn't pay any attention to her. She hated it when she acted this way.

"Yeah, right, Mom." Karla fought the urge to scream at her. All she could do was glare and her mom didn't even seem to notice this either.

She thought about how many times her mom didn't appear to know she existed. Karla decided she'd start blowing her off the way she did to her.

We'll see how she likes it, she thought to herself. She wanted to flip her mother off so badly, but she feared the outcome.

"Hey, I got to get going," said Sarah. "I've to meet Barry at the town field for soccer practice. Here is my cell phone number." Sarah reached into her front pocket, producing a piece of paper. "I got to go, or I'll be late. Talk to you soon."

Numb with anger at her mom's response, Karla handed the phone back to Sarah, accepting the piece of paper; she stuffed it in her pocket. Sarah quickly said good-bye, and how she hated to have to run, but she'd to go.

Frustrated by her mom's response, Karla gave the ground a swift kick with her foot after Sarah left. She shook her head and went back inside the house to her room. She was sure no one would notice her missing.

She slammed her bedroom door closed behind her and flicked on her stereo to a hip-hop radio station. She turned up the volume, trying to drown out the sounds of the party.

Throwing herself onto her bed face first, Karla buried her face into her pillow and began to sob.

# 3

THE NEXT FOUR DAYS WERE AGONIZING FOR KARLA. THE PACKING and preparing for the move was trying. Her mother kept checking to make sure she was packing her things and packing them properly. Was there any other way to pack? She wasn't just throwing her stuff in the boxes as her mom seemed to fear.

The boxes just kept stacking up in front of her closet. It got to the point where she no longer able to open her closet. The boxes were in the way.

On Tuesday, her dad took her to the new school she was transferring. She was impressed with the size of the school, at the same time the size of it intimidated her. Karla feared she wouldn't be able to find her way around and would be wandering aimlessly through the hallways, always late for her classes.

After they'd registered her at her new school, she'd to finish the packing. She was glad that her mom didn't accompany them to have her transferred to the school. Karla was sure she would've embarrassed her in front of staff and students by fussing over her classes she chose to take.

Karla also spent all day Wednesday packing too. She not only had to pack up her bedroom, but she needed to help her mom pack up the kitchen. Then her dad had her help him with the basement.

Karla had many bitter disputes with her mother. Her mom kept criticizing her, saying she was not wrapping the dishes enough. She fought the tears each time her mom started yelling at her.

Thursday was the big day. The day they were finally moving to Brantwood. Karla was so happy to be done with all the packing. Next, the chore of loading all the things in the U-Haul was here.

"Okay, that was the last box," her dad said with enthusiasm. "Everyone in the truck and wave good-bye, Karla, you're going to love your new room."

Karla complained some more about the move and climbed into the back slumping against the seat of the moving van with crossed arms in protest.

Her dad glared at her. "Karla stop it! I'm not going to listen to your whining all the way there. We're moving, and that's final." He slammed the truck door closed.

"Just give it a chance, Karla." Her mom chided as she climbed into the passenger seat.

Karla remained slouched in the back seat. Biting her lip, she fought the tears she that were beginning to pool in her eyes. The house was now empty. All her memories were still in that house both dear ones and sad ones.

Her dad started up the truck. They slowly drove away and down the street. They passed Little Amy. She stood holding on to her bike with one hand while she was waving to them with her other hand.

They passed Jan in her Honda. She pulled into her driveway with a load of groceries. She'd remembered to give Karla the recipe for the ambrosia yesterday.

It seemed like a half an hour had passed before they entered the town of Brantwood. It was some twenty miles away from their small town of Medham.

Karla sat with her arms crossed for most of the way. When they entered the city of Brantwood, she leaned forward against the front seat, trying to see what the new place looked like.

It was a small city.

The houses were sparsely scattered along both sides of the road. They clustered closer and closer together as they traveled toward the center of town. Several traffic lights lined the street slowing the cars down to a crawl.

Her dad announced beaming with excitement as soon as they were about to reach the first landmark of importance to Karla, "This is it, your new town, the city of Brantwood. Over there is the way to your new school, Brantwood High." He pointed.

They'd driven for a bit more before he said each different landmark. "There's the mall and movie theater... Library, and over there is the bowling alley, we're almost there. Oh and there are a lot of one-way streets in this town."

They drove passed a mini mart on a corner and turned down the next street. Their new home was sandwiched on a side street between the mall and the school. One was in one direction, and the other was in the other direction.

Karla's dad pulled into the left turn lane at a stoplight.

The bustle of cars and pedestrians had her attention.

Karla watched an elderly woman dressed in drab clothes push a small shopping cart along the sidewalk. She was one of those homeless persons. The woman then stopped when she got to the crosswalk to wait for the light to change. Karla continued to watch as this woman began to push the button on the pole repeatedly in hopes of making the light switch faster.

Her dad turned the corner and announced, "This is our street..." The sound of his voice brought Karla's attention back to the road ahead of her.

She noted where the mini mart was and how close it was to their street. Maybe she could walk to it in the next few days to buy some candy or something.

The library was not far away either. They passed a church as they turned down their new street.

"Mom, did you ask Dad about the cell phone?" Karla was still leaning forward against the front seats so she could see the landmarks of interest.

Her mom scowled, "I haven't had a chance to, we've been so busy."

She gave her mom a quick sneer behind her back.

"Karla, I'll look into getting you one, but only if you promise to stop complaining about our having to move. We didn't want to have to do this either. But we've to do what we've to do." Mr. Centon responded, frustrated by Karla's constant whining, and the tension between Karla and her mom. He also gave her mom a glaring side look to that her mom didn't see.

Their house was the tenth house down the street on the left. Her mom's blue sedan was already sitting in the driveway. She wondered what time her parents got up this morning. Karla didn't recall hearing her mom leave, but she knew the car was gone.

Her mom said excitedly, "This is it."

Mr. Centon backed the moving truck into the driveway, parking it beside her mom's car. A small gray cat scooted across the street, darting toward the house next door.

Karla waited impatiently to get out of the truck. She let her eyes scan over the outside of the new home. It looked similar to the last house they were living in. Just, not as many trees around the property and the houses were much closer together. She couldn't see into the back yard from where she stood, a tall wooden fence blocked her view.

"Where's the pool. Can I see the pool?" Karla said. "Everyone keeps saying we have a pool now."

"It's around back. Hurry back, there's a lot to do and not much time," her dad replied while he opened the door to the back of the truck and pulled out the ramp. He untied a moving dolly from the inside of the van. This was what he was going to use to bring big stacks of boxes into the house.

He shoved its base underneath a stack of boxes, pulled them off the truck and wheeled them into the house.

"Yeah... I'll be right back, Dad. I just want to take a quick look." Karla found the latch on the wooden fence and made her way out behind the house.

She grinned at the sight of the in-ground pool. It took up a large portion of the half-acre backyard. A patio centered by the pool and the house. Now she knew why Jan kept talking about pool parties.

A tall fence blocking her view of the neighborhood surrounded the backyard. She noted the pool was empty, not even a puddle was seen in the bottom of it. Karla ran back to help her dad with the boxes. Her mood significantly changed for the better. Most people love having a pool and Karla was one of them.

"Dad, how come there's no water in the pool," she asked as she grabbed some of the boxes from the truck.

"The last owners drained it last fall," Mr. Centon explained. "The house has been vacant since winter. We're going to leave it empty, too, for now. We'll fill it next summer, have it ready for Memorial Day."

Karla was impressed knowing she now had an in-ground pool. She liked the idea of not having to worry about bloodsuckers anymore. Too bad, it wouldn't have any water in it until next summer. That was okay with her, and the backyard was large enough to have cookouts and pool parties. The thought of the pool parties left a small smile on her face.

Maybe the pool would help her become a little bit more popular in her new school. Every girl wants to be relatively popular with her classmates. It makes life easier when no one is bullying you every day at school.

Karla carried a box in her arms as she stepped up a couple of cement steps leading into the house. Looking around as she entered the sunken living room of what must've been a garage at one time. She didn't care for the color of the old wallpaper on its walls. It made it seem so odd with the swirls and off color.

"Yuck... What awful wallpaper," Karla commented.

Her mom looked up from a box she was digging in that was in on the breakfast nook separating the dining room from the kitchen.

"I've to agree, that's going to be one of the first projects your dad will be tackling. That wallpaper does have to go, along with the rest of the wallpaper."

"Good... cause I can't stand it."

Karla stepped up the steps leading to the kitchen and the rest of the house and asked, "Mom, where do you want me to put these?" Her mood had significantly changed after seeing the pool and no longer spoke to her mom with an attitude.

"Right over there." Her mom motioned to a corner of the room where the dining room table would be going.

"Where's my room," Karla asked as she placed the box down on the floor.

"You go get another box, and I'll show you your room," her mom bargained with her.

This was no longer necessary. Karla didn't care. Even her mom now sounded a little bit happier than usual, which was always a plus. It was much better than having her mom bark orders at her all the time.

Karla spotted the case of soda on the kitchen counter. "Okay." She stopped to get one each. One for her and one for her dad. Pausing before she returned to get another box, she let her eyes quickly scan the kitchen. It was plentiful with cabinets, with an almond colored refrigerator and stove. The kitchen window and sliding glass door looked out at the swimming pool in the back yard which caught her attention for a brief moment.

After quickly looking around the kitchen for the first time, she paused in the living room, on her way back outside to help her dad with the truckload. She stopped to take another quick peek at the living room and avoided looking at the wallpaper. Karla was happy to see the fireplace. She'd always wished for one just like the one Jody's parents had.

She skipped out the door, bringing the soda for her dad. "Thought you might like something to drink," Karla said as she handed him his soda.

"Thanks..." Her dad accepted the can, cracking the tab and waiting for the bubbles to settle before taking a sip.

Karla made several trips into the house carrying armfuls of boxes. Her dad used the moving dolly, loading stacks of boxes onto it so he wouldn't have to make many trips, pulling the dolly up the stairs backward to get them into the house.

Her dad struggled with a couple loads of boxes. Karla had to help him by lifting up on the bottom of the dolly to get it up the cement steps and into the house. Some of them were apparently substantial in weight.

"What's in these boxes?" Karla asked.

"Books... I forgot we'd so many until I started packing them."

"We can put the bookcase over here," her mom, pointed to a bare wall in the dining room.

"All right... The furniture is coming in next anyway. That was the last of the boxes." Mr. Centon motioned for Karla to follow him back outside. "Come on Karla, we've furniture to bring in and then we'll be done."

Karla found some of the furniture big and bulky, like the sofa and mattresses. She tried to carry them in the house going backward, but she stumble going up the stairs, so she traded sides with her dad. This made it easier for her.

A group of teens gathered across the street to watch them move into the house. Karla was conscious of their eyes on her. She was motivated by the onlookers from across the street and at the same time she began wondering what grade they were in and if they went to her school. Were there more kids her age living on her street?

Karla's bedroom furniture was the last things off the truck. She'd been waiting for what seemed hours to see her new bedroom. It looked a little bit bigger than her last room. Again, wallpaper smothered the walls with ugly swirls.

"Eh. God. What ugly colors."

Her dad set his end of her bureau against the wall of her room. "Sometime soon I'll rent a steam cleaner, and we'll strip your walls."

Karla pointed to the swirls on the wall. "Good. Cause this is gay."

"We're done now with unloading the truck. You can start setting up your room the way you want it. We'll be back in a bit. Your mom and I've to return the truck."

Karla nodded. She pushed her stripped bed up against the wall under one of the two windows. She looked out and saw the group of teenagers was gone. Her dad was pulling out of the driveway with the truck, followed behind by her mom in the sedan.

She then began setting herself to her new task and started looking for all the boxes with her name on them. She'd made sure she'd written her name on the sides of all the boxes that she'd packed in for her room. After several minutes of searching, she found them stacked in the dining room next to the pile of boxes containing the books.

She decided to carry them to her room one at a time. Taking care, Karla avoided stacking them against her closet. She needed to be able to hang some of her clothes. The third box she came across were clothes for her bureau. When she opened her top drawer of her dresser to put her underwear away, she found a wrapped package.

Picking up the package, she saw the note card. It read: We hope this helps you with your transition to your new school, love Mom and Dad. "Oh my God, did they actually get me one? It can't be."

Karla ripped the gift-wrap off the package exposing the box label LG with a photo of a cell phone on it. She wanted to jump for joy. She opened the box and sat down on her still unmade bed. She hadn't found her box with her bedding yet. It was probably going to be the last box she came across.

She couldn't wait to see what her phone was like. She pulled it from the box and began fumbling through its contents. She set several items onto her bed, the charger, the battery, and a holder for the phone. Karla then found the instruction booklet and glanced through it, looking to see what features her phone had.

It had caller ID, call waiting, texting, wi-fi, and most importantly a camera. Now she'd be able to take pictures of her school and send them to Sarah and Jody.

Happy with her discovery, she decided to set it on top of her bureau. She'd come back to it later. There were still more boxes she needed to bring into her room, and the phone needed to be charged. She decided this would be a decent place to keep the phone while it was charging.

She then made several more trips to the dining room to get the rest of her boxes. As she picked up the last box, she heard the sound of a couple of cars pulling into the driveway. She recognized the sound of her parent's cars and stood there waiting for them to enter the house.

When they entered the house, Karla decided to take the last box into her room. She returned quickly with her new phone in her hand. She knew they'd be expecting a big thank you. "Oh my God, you got me a cell phone?"

Karla was still ecstatic with excitement and gave her mom a gigantic hug, "Thank you. Thank you so much, Mom."

Mrs. Centon smiled she was apparently pleased with Karla's change in attitude, "Don't thank me, thank your dad. He picked it out last night." Her mom returned the hug. "But, I do hope you like it."

"Dad, thank you for the phone," Karla hugged her dad too. "I got to go call Sarah."

"You're welcome, but for now on I don't want to hear any more whining about our having to move away from your friends."

He returned the hug.

## 4

FRIDAY MORNING CAME FAST FOR KARLA. SHE'D SPENT A COUPLE OF hours searching for her bedding. Ten o'clock had rolled around before she was able to make her bed. This was after she unpacked her last box of school clothes and hung them in her closet, making it late when she went to bed.

"Karla? Are you up?" Her Mom's voice vibrated through her body and shocked her out of a sound sleep. She rolled over to look at the alarm clock.

Argh. She groaned to herself. "Yeah," Karla answered. She turned over in her bed, pulling the blanket over her head. She muttered softly to herself, "Morning already?"

"Do you want anything for breakfast," her mom hollered through the closed door.

Karla growled in annoyance. Her mom yelling at her through the closed door bugged her. "No! Mom."

She sat up in bed and waited to come to here senses. She'd hoped that the move was just a nightmare. When she opened her eyes, there were still some unpacked boxes piled along the bedroom wall. They confirmed the move had been the real thing.

"How 'bout hot chocolate," her mom prodded. She was still calling through Karla's closed bedroom door.

"No, Mom," Karla growled again.

She forced herself out of bed and began gathering the clothes she was going to wear. It was her first day at her new school, and she wanted to wear one of her new outfits. She searched through the ones hanging in her closet, pushing them one way and then pulling them back until she settled for a blue t-shirt and a pair of jeans.

"Glass of milk," her mom offered once again through the closed door.

"No, Mom," Karla groaned.

"Coffee," her mom offered.

"NO! MOM. I'm getting dressed, and I'll be out in a minute," Karla snapped.

"Well, you don't need to talk to me like that. I just wanted to fix you something before you went to school," her mom griped.

"I don't need or want anything." God, why doesn't she just leave me alone?

Karla slipped into her shirt and pants and then she snatched a pair of socks from the top bureau drawer and shoved them onto her feet. Jamming her feet into her untied sneakers, she left her bedroom, with her bedroom door shut behind her, hiding her unmade bed. Her untied laces clicked on the wood floor as she walked.

Typically, Karla's mom wouldn't even bother with offering her any breakfast. The fact that her mom kept insisting on her having something was in itself irritating. She also thought it was weird that her mom was even up at this hour. Usually, Karla would get herself up and off to school while her mom kept right on sleeping, probably from a nights worth of heavy drinking of vodka and tomato juice.

Her mom hadn't gotten up to make her breakfast since she'd been in first grade. That hadn't lasted for more than a week. At the age of six, Karla would get herself up and ready for school all by herself. If she missed the bus, her mom would threaten to ground her for a month.

She only missed the bus once, which was enough to teach Karla that that was not such an admirable thing to do. Her mom yelled at her all the way to school for making her get up out of bed so early in the morning.

"Just remember, I offered," her mom called once again from the kitchen.

Karla followed the short hallway to the kitchen. Her bedroom was again across the hall from the bathroom, just as her parents' bedroom was also once again located at the end of the hallway. The house was pretty much the same layout as before except for the fact that the living room was sunken this time instead of being on the same floor level.

She entered the kitchen taking a couple slices of bread and slipped them into the toaster. Then she grabbed a glass and poured herself some juice.

"I thought you didn't want anything," her mom protested.

"Eh. I changed my mind …okay," Karla growled. She wondered what was up with her mom pushing breakfast on her anyway. She was weird today.

"What's with the attitude," her mom chided, "You better change it."

"God, Mom. I don't have an attitude. Just stop bugging me." Karla moved away from the kitchen sink so her dad could set his empty coffee cup down. She sat down at the breakfast nook to eat her toast while her dad gave her the look. He'd stepped in between her and her mom. He ran his hand over his balding head.

"Karla, there is no more riding the bus from now on," he announced. "So, you've your choice this morning; you can either walk to school, or I can drop you off on my way to work," he said while he straightened his tie.

Karla thought he looked too funny wearing a suit and tie. She snickered to herself while she watched him try to button up his suit coat. The buttons over his stomach were so tight, they were ready to pop. She'd no idea what his job was, but he appeared to be dressed as a salesman.

"Kay, Dad. I'll ride with you this time," answered Karla. She was happy to escape her mom's pestering. The first-day jitters formed in her stomach. She nibbled another bite of toast.

"Well, you need to get your things, then because I'm leaving now," he said while he picked up his briefcase. He didn't wait for Karla. Instead, he headed toward the door and paused long enough to take his lunch bag and coffee cup on his way out.

"Ah… I just made the toast," Karla stammered.

"Drink your juice up, and you can take your toast with you. Eat it in the car," he said on his way out the front door to start the car.

On his way out, he stopped to kiss her mom goodbye. Karla was not used to seeing her parents kiss, even just a little peck. Most times, they were glaring at each other instead.

"Okay, I'm coming," she called after him. Karla grabbed her backpack and slung it over her shoulder. Quickly, she drained her glass of juice and placed the empty glass in the sink. She then gathered up her toast in a paper towel and followed her dad out the door.

She was not used to living so close to the school. It only took about five minutes to make the trip. This was only because they had to wait for the streetlight at the end of their street. Other than that, they would've been there sooner.

"Do you know where to go," her dad asked as they pulled up in front of the school entrance. He put the car in park and waited for Karla to gather her things.

"Dad you don't need to hold my hand, I'm not a little kid anymore." Karla could feel her frustration coming back. Parents could be so annoying. She glanced out the car window and saw a group of students gathered outside the entrance. The butterflies flopped around in her stomach. The last thing she needed was her dad to escort her into a school in front of all these kids.

Her dad smiled at her. "Just checking to make sure you're set to do this by yourself."

"I can do it, Dad," she reassured him.

Karla scooped up her backpack and stuffed the leftover toast into the pocket of her hoodie. She couldn't finish her toast right now, the butterflies made her stomach to queasy.

"All right…I'll see you tonight at supper. Good luck on your first day," her dad said to her as she opened the car door.

"Thanks, Dad. See yah later."

Karla could feel the eyes of other students watching her as she shut the car door. She stood on the sidewalk for a brief moment and watched her dad drive off. She then turned around, walked up the school steps, and passed the onlookers gathered by the entrance. A catcall sounded off to her right, and she ignored this as she entered. Once inside, Karla's eyes passed over the array of bulletin boards on two of the walls.

There was a trophy case with a school banner strung above it. The lobby connected to three corridors. There was one off to the left, one straight ahead, and the other off to the right. She spotted the office straight ahead on the right. It sat between two of the corridors.

Karla entered the office, walked right up to the counter, and waited for the secretary. She stood at the counter while other students came and dropped off papers. The morning bell rang bringing a bustle of students who were hurrying past the office windows.

Trays of various papers were stacked on top of the right side of the counter where it attached to the wall. The walls covered with several posters. One of the posters had to do with a college fair while the other two were advertising for the armed forces.

"Hi. I'm new here. I was told to stop by here and get a copy of my schedule," Karla piped up as soon as the secretary stepped into the room and noticed her standing there waiting.

"What's the name?"

"Karla Centon"

"Just a sec... Oh, here it is... found it. Here is a map of the school, just in case you need it. And here is a pass for your first class, if you should get lost." The secretary paused for a moment when a student entered the office and then spoke to her. "Oh, Carol. Are you on your way to Miss Brangton's history class?"

"Yeah"

"Would you be kind enough to show Karla here to class," the secretary asked Carol. "She's new here, and she happens to be in your history class." She handed the schedule and a map to Karla.

"Yeah, I guess," answered Carol. She sounded like she'd better things to do than to show Karla around.

Carol picked up some papers off the counter and led Karla out into the hall. Most of the students were now in their classes emptying out the hallway.

Karla followed Carol silently along the corridor. Her eyes took in the art murals on the corridor walls, amazed by the skill of the artist. She thought to herself how this wasn't ever allowed in Medham High. What fabulous artwork.

Carol broke the silence. "I've to stop at my locker and pick up my book. Where's your locker?"

"Oh...I don't know." Karla was jolted back to the here and now by the sound of Carol's voice. She looked down at the paper she held in her hand.

"Let me see." Carol took the paper from Karla. "Oh, I know where that one is. Over here, just a couple down from mine." She handed it back to Karla and opened her own locker.

"Thanks." Karla looked for her locker number on her paper. "4551... Right. Found it. Great combo lockers, I hate those types. I always forget the combo." She began trying the combination to her locker.

"Come on, you can mess with the combo later. We got to go, or we'll be late for class." Carol slammed her locker shut. She beckoned Karla to follow her.

"Hey, Carol. Talk to me later," the red headed girl shouted to Carol as they passed each other in the hallway. They walked down the hall a bit more before taking a right into another wing of the school. Karla saw a blonde approach shouting as they made their way down the corridor.

"Carol... call me." A girl with dark complexion passed them next and shouted, "Carol. What time is practice till?"

Carol turned around and walked backward, answering her, "I'll get back to you."

Stopping short before a room on the left, Carol scooted into the class. "Here it is. You can sit wherever, we don't have assigned seats." She set her book down on her own desk.

Karla moved to take a seat near Carol. She was unsure of how this school was going to agree with her. Some of the things, like the wall art, she thought was decent. What she didn't like was how the school was so big, and the classes being so spread out making her have to hurry to each class if she wanted to get to them on time.

"Oh, you can't sit there."

Carol riveted Karla out of her deep thought.

"That where Donna sits."

She looked around and pointed to another empty desk across the room. "Hey, that one has been empty; you can sit there."

"You must be Karla," Miss Brangton said as she entered the room. She closed the door behind her.

"Yes," Karla answered softly. She turned around to see who was addressing her.

"I'm Miss Brangton," she replied, "Yes; it is safe to sit there," Miss Brangton nodded her approval.

She then turned to address the class, "Class, we have a new student with us. Her name is Karla Centon. Why don't we all welcome her and help her find her way around the school?"

A guy two desks over to the right turned around in his seat. His gray eyes met Karla's brown eyes. His blonde, shoulder-length hair had small wisps of ringlets on both sides of his head.

"Oh God. He's cute," Karla thought to herself.

She could feel her cheeks grow warm as their eyes locked onto each other. As soon as he turned back, to face the front of the class she was able to sit back in her seat and relax.

Karla fought the smile and ran her hand through her hair. Her heart wanted to jump right up into her throat. He was gorgeous, and he'd noticed her. She never ever thought a guy would notice her, especially on her first day.

Nervously, she pushed her books to the left corner of her desk. Karla couldn't keep herself from looking in his direction all through class. She had a hard time focusing on her teacher. Occasionally she'd catch him taking quick glances at her over his shoulder. This would make her smile even more.

At the end of class, Carol caught Karla by her arm. "Karla? What's your next class?"

"Math," Karla answered, looking down at her schedule. She read to herself, "Math, lunch, Digital Imaging, English, and last, Biology. Hmm. I can't wait to see what Digital Imaging will be like."

"Oh, I got science. It's in the opposite direction. If you want, you can sit with us during lunch. You do have first lunch, right," Carol babbled quickly as she followed Karla out the door.

"Yeah, I guess I do," Karla answered, surprised by the lunch invitation. The only ones she'd ever eaten lunch with had been Sarah and Jody. They always sat at a table by themselves away from the rest of the big cliques.

"Later, at lunch then," Carol called behind her. She followed the cute guy down the hall.

"See yah," Karla replied. She just couldn't take her eyes off the guy. She stood mesmerized. Carol kept chattering about something to him while they walked away down the hallway until they were out of Karla's sight.

The day seemed to be off to a great start. A cute guy had taken notice of her, and now she'd a lunch invitation. Maybe this was going to be a decent school after all.

# 5

KARLA FOLLOWED THE ROOM NUMBERS ON THE DOORS. PASSING another corridor, she was sure she'd get lost by the end of the day.

"This school is big," she muttered to herself, careful no one else heard her while she wandered about looking for her next class.

She finally found the room for her next class, math, making it into the room just as the bell rang. Looking around, Karla found the teacher standing at the back of the room. She made her way past occupied desks to greet him.

Making eye contact, Mr. Petradona smiled at Karla. "Hi, you must be Karla. We've been expecting you."

"Hi," Karla replied. The eye contact bothered her. She'd to look away.

"Damn. Does he have to stare," she wondered to herself. He certainly made her feel uneasy with the way he looked at her.

She followed his gaze while he looked around the room. Mr. Petradona spotted an empty desk for Karla. "Oh, you can have this desk over here by the window."

She set her bag on the floor next to her desk and sat down in the chair. Karla waited while Mr. Petradona found her a textbook. After he had written down the book number in his paperwork, he gave her the book.

"Class, we'll be moving to the next chapter; Geometry."

"Oh yeah, I'm just thrilled to death. Who needs geometry, anyway?" Again she muttered to herself.

Karla obliged and opened her book to the chapter on geometry, this lead to watching the clock on the wall. The time just seemed to go by so slowly. Her mind began to wander back to that cute guy in history.

Ten minutes to twelve, he finally wrote the homework assignment on the board. Karla quickly jotted it down, checking out the pages in her book. She slipped her book into her bag just as the bell rang.

Before leaving the classroom, Karla pulled out the map of the school to see where the cafeteria was located. It was down the corridor she'd passed on her way to her math class. She stuffed the map back into her bag and swung it over her shoulder, making her way to the cafeteria.

Karla noticed groups of students going in the same direction she was going in. She decided to follow them. They lead her to the cafeteria. Looking around the cafeteria, Karla found Carol sitting at a table by the windows. She hoped Carol would still let her eat lunch with her.

Boldly, Karla walked over to Carol's table. Carol looked up as she approached. "Hi," Karla called out, hopeful that the invitation still stood.

"Karla, come sit with us," Carol invited.

"Sure," Karla accepted. She saw the empty spots at the other end of the table and started to make her way to one of them, but Carol stopped her.

"Darcy, let Karla have your seat today," Carol demanded of one of her friends who happened to sit directly across the table from her.

Karla stopped and watched as Darcy moved to the other end of the table. She was not expecting them to do that for her. She took Darcy's place at the table, hoping the girl wouldn't be angry with her for taking her place.

"So, Karla, what do you think of this school," Carol asked. She picked up her bottle of Gatorade and swigged some down. "Hey, Maggie, are you gonna eat that?"

Karla watched as a short, short brown haired girl handed Carol her sandwich. She saw several others also give a portion of their lunch to Carol.

Karla didn't know she was giving Carol a questioning, that's until Carol said defensively, "What? So I forgot my lunch money. Give me a break."

Karla shrugged the odd behavior off. She took out her own lunch and began to eat it. A bag of chips sat on the table before her. She pondered whether to offer the chips to her or not.

"Want my chips?" Karla asked Carol. Carol shook her head. Karla picked up the bag intended to eat them.

"I'll have them."

Karla turned her attention toward the person who'd spoken up to see who was asking for her chips. She saw whom it was, the cute guy from history. Her face grew hot as she gave him the chips. He grinned as her eyes locked on his once again. She forced herself to break the connection and looked away quickly.

"I don't know if I'm gonna like this school? It's humongous. It takes too long to get to your classes," Karla answered Carol. She had a hard time not looking in the cute guy's direction.

"What school did you go to?" Carol asked after chewing a bite of the sandwich Maggie had given her. She then washed it down with another gulp of the Gatorade.

Karla washed her own mouthful down before responding. "Medham High."

"That's a small school. I've been there for the football games. My boyfriend, Heath, is on our football team," Carol smiled, obviously she was proud of him.

Karla said nothing. She went on eating her sandwich. Suddenly she realized that was where she'd seen her before, at one of the football games.

Carol broke the silence between them after taking another sip of her drink, she asked, "What classes did you take?"

Karla glanced down the other end of the table before answering Carol. The boys were flipping chips back and forth at each other from the bag she'd given to the cute guy. Karla snickered to herself, thinking of how childish they were behaving.

"The usual; English, math, science, history, Digital Imaging, gym, you know, crap courses," Karla answered, bringing her attention back to Carol.

Carol tossed her trash on Maggie's lunch tray and turned back to Karla, she asked, "Any after-school activities?"

"No..." Karla raised an eyebrow, surprised by the inquiry, and wondered to herself who stays after school these days.

Carol capped her empty bottle and handed it off to Darcy to throw away for her. "Interested in volleyball?"

"Never thought about it before," Karla answered, taken aback by the question. Gym and exercise weren't her favorite subjects.

"We've tryouts next week," Carol invited. She leaned toward Maggie to whisper something into her ear. Maggie smiled approvingly.

"Well, that leaves me out. The only time I've ever played volleyball was during gym. And that wasn't terribly often." The whispering and sly smiles made Karla feel extremely uncomfortable. She began to wonder if they were whispering about her.

"That's okay, we can teach you," Maggie offered. Her straight brown hair hung almost to her shoulders.

"I don't know...I'm not that coordinated," Karla answered. She was trying to back out of the conversation as best as she could. Her and sports just never mixed.

"Well, we can teach you for next year. You're a sophomore right?" Darcy pitched in. Karla hadn't noticed she'd taken the empty seat next to her. The sudden appearance startled her.

"Yeah," Karla tried not to sound too leery. She began to think they were kind of pushy, and she couldn't help wondering what all the whispering was all about.

"We can get you ready for JV. You should give it a try," Carol encouraged one last time. She looked up at the clock and began to gather her things.

"I'll think about it," Karla relented. She took Carol's clue and took her leftover lunch to the trash. Looking at the clock on the wall, she saw lunch was almost over.

"Karla, what's your next class," Carol asked as the bell rang. She flipped open a cell phone to check for messages. Finding none, she flipped it closed and pocketed the phone.

Karla had to dig out her schedule again, "Digital Imaging." She stuffed the schedule back into her bag after taking a peek at the map. Which she quickly replaced in her bag since she didn't want anyone to know she'd no clue as to where to go next.

"Well, I got to go. Maybe I'll see you later," Carol bade goodbye and left with her friends.

"I'll see yah," Karla called out after her. She watched as Carol met up with Heath in the hallway. The two of them stopped on the side of the hall for a quick kiss.

Karla pondered over the awkwardness of the conversation about volleyball tryouts. She was surprised that lunch went so well, but all that whispering certainly did bother her.

Karla was lost in thought while she walked down the hall toward her Digital Imaging class. A couple of upper classmen who were in a hurry to get to their next class bumped into her, causing her to have a near run-in with Gerry. All because she was not paying attention to the people around her.

She jumped when she almost bumped into him. The cute guy had stopped at his locker. She'd to sidestep quickly to avoid him. Blushing again, she quickly hurried on her way.

I hope no one saw that, especially him, she thought to herself when she looked over her shoulder to see if she was being watched. He looked in her direction and smiled at her. Her face went beet red. Oh, God. I know he must've seen that. She tucked her head down and hurried to her class.

All morning Carol had been gibbering about some new girl who'd started today to both Darcy and Maggie. This was going to be another girl they harassed until she either convinced her parents into moving back to where they came from or sent her to some private school.

The idea was to get her to try out for the volleyball team, and once she was on it, they'd rough her up some during the practices. A little bit of bullying usually went a long way when it came to intimidating the new kid.

But Carol hadn't bothered to mention how Gerry had taken a liking to the new girl, Karla. Maggie saw the way he looked at her during lunch. This was after Darcy pointed it out to her. There was no way she was going to stand for this. He was supposed to be her man, no one else's, especially the new girl. If she couldn't have him, no one could've him.

It was apparent to Maggie and Darcy that Gerry liked Karla by the way he looked at her. She was pretty, but that made no difference to Maggie, she was going to see to it that the two of them never happened. If that meant that Maggie had to get rid of Karla herself, then that was what she was going to do it.

Gerry was her man, and he was going to stay her man.

# 6

THE LAST BELL OF THE DAY RANG. KARLA FINISHED WRITING DOWN the homework assignment that was on the board at the back of the class. The textbook and notebook she stuffed into her bag and slung it over her shoulder, leaving the room.

Karla found the hallway busy with students heading to their lockers. Some students had stopped in groups to chat with friends while others stopped at their lockers to stash unneeded books. She wove in and out of the crowd toward the main doors.

Once outside, Karla saw Carol standing at the entrance. She appeared to be waving at her while her friends were walking away. Karla thought maybe she was waiting for her or maybe someone else. She nodded to Carol when she passed where she stood.

"Karla. What're you doing after school today," Carol called out, stopping Karla from walking by. She'd once again reached out and grabbed Karla by the elbow.

Karla thought it was strange of Carol to stop her, instead of going with her friends. No one waits for the new kid. Not even at Karla's old school, no one ever did that.

"Um… I guess unpacking, other than that, nothing. Why," Karla responded.

"I was wondering if you wanted to hang out with me today." Carol dug her lipgloss out of her purse and began applying it.

"I don't know…I still have a lot of unpacking to do."

Karla was leery of the invitation. All the whispering at lunchtime was still fresh in her mind. She was not sure she should trust Carol. She'd a sudden gut feeling.

"How about this weekend," Carol smiled, her long blonde hair blowing in the breeze.

"I really don't know. Do you have a phone? I can call you if I can take off for a while," Karla replied. She was trying to come up with excuses.

"Yeah," Carol wrote her number down on an envelope she took from her purse. "Here, call me."

Karla couldn't help noticing the clutter filling the purse when she opened it.

"Here's my cell phone number." Karla had taken a page from her notebook so she could exchange phone numbers with her. She then slung her backpack back up on her shoulder and began to walk away from Carol.

Carol started to follow her down the street. She actually didn't mind the company. Karla never had to walk to and from school before.

"Oh, cool, you got a cell phone," Carol sounded impressed while gazing at the paper Karla had handed her. Shoving it in her purse, she walked in stride with Karla.

"Yeah, my folks just got it for me. I'm still learning how to text with it," Karla giggled, thinking of how she loved her new phone. It just had so many functions to learn. It had games, and it could take pictures.

"I'd one, but it died today," Carol replied glumly, "I accidentally dropped it and now it won't work. I got to get me a new one."

They passed the corner store. Carol disappeared for a moment. Karla thought she'd gone a different way. She reappeared just as fast as she'd disappeared. Karla shrugged it off. They walked for about two blocks and turned down a side street.

"This is my house. Maybe I'll see you later. I'll call if I've time to hang out with you," Karla announced as she stopped in front of her driveway.

"Sounds good," responded Carol. She turned around to go back in the direction they'd come in.

Thinking about how weird the walk home was, Karla looked back to see Carol was already up to the end of the street. She turned the corner and disappeared from sight.

Before Karla came out of the school Carol, Darcy and Maggie agreed that they needed to do what they always did to the new kids coming into their school, especially the girls.

Most of the time, just by harassing them they usually wound up moving away or going to a different school because they were intimidated.

Carol thought Maggie was right. They didn't need to be losing their men to some chick from some other school. Even though Carol was sure that Karla was not Heath's type. But just the same, Maggie did have a point.

So Carol agreed they should find out first where Karla lived and then they'd go from there to see how they were going to go about intimidating her into leaving their school system.

She waited patiently for Karla to come out the school. It seemed odd to her that Karla was just going to pass her by like she wasn't anyone of importance. She was just going to have to make sure this new girl knew she should be respected.

Getting her to stop to talk to her took some effort on Carol's part. This typically didn't happen this way with the new kids. Most of them would be jumping at the chance to be friends with Carol and her clique.

This new girl might be difficult. Maybe she too was a bully at her other school. Carol would just have to find out for herself. She decided to ask her to hang out with her. This was the best way to find out what a person was like, just by getting to know them.

When she asked her, Karla sounded like she was trying to blow her off.

This new girl was making her curious. No one ever blew her off, not Darcy or Maggie, no one dared, except Karla dared. Maybe this new girl was different in some way. Maybe the two of them had more in common than she thought.

As agreed, Carol followed Karla home to find out where she lived. If need be, they could resort to vandalism to intimidate the new girl's family.

When they stopped in front of Karla's house, Carol was surprised to see where she was living. It was the house with the in-ground pool.

That was where Janus had lived. Her family moved down south last year after Janus entered her first year in college. She never had heard which college she'd gone to just that she'd gotten a four-year scholarship for volleyball.

Janus had brought the Brantwood Volleyball team into its first-ever state championship.

When Carol laid eyes on where Karla was living, she began to think of alternative ideas. Mostly about parties, pool parties to be exact. Everyone loves pool parties, including Darcy and Maggie.

Maybe this new girl wasn't going to be so bad after all. They were just going to have to test her and see what she does. They'd have to watch her around Gerry for Maggie's sake, even if Gerry weren't one bit interested in Maggie to begin with.

Everyone knew Maggie was somewhat crazy. She was a stalker and a nut job with crazy delusional ideas. Even Gerry knew, that's why he refused to go out with her.

Maggie had been pissed off by this ever since.

# 7

"HI, KARLA HOW WAS YOUR DAY," HER MOM GREETED HER AS SHE walked through the door.

"All right," Karla set her backpack down on the floor in the kitchen. She'd been in a good mood up until now. Opening the fridge, she helped herself to a can of soda. Her mom still seemed to be acting weird. First, this morning with the badgering of breakfast items and now she was hovering over her in the kitchen. Was she sober at this time of the day?

"Was that a new friend," asked her mom.

Karla braced herself for the ten million-question quiz. She could sense it was coming. She took a couple more gulps of her orange soda before responding.

"Just a girl I met in school today," she said nonchalantly. Karla wished her mom worked like most moms, and then she wouldn't be here when she got home from school with her ten million questions.

"Does she live down the street," her mom went on asking.

Karla drank more of her soda, making it half empty before she reached for the cookie jar to take one. After taking a bite, she responded, "Yeah, Mom."

"What's her name?"

Her mom was really starting to irritate her with all these questions. She looked at the clock her dad had hung on the wall above the kitchen sink. Wishing she'd found a longer way to walk home from school. Maybe Monday she'd try taking a different route, just to kill some time.

"Carol. Her name is Carol. Stop, Mom," Karla couldn't take any more of her mother's questions, "Stop asking so many questions." She picked up her backpack and slung it over her shoulder. With the soda in her right hand and the cookies clutched in the other, she decided to escape to her bedroom.

"I just wanted to know how your day went," her mom called after her.

"Well, it went okay…I'm going to go finish unpacking," she replied as she opened her bedroom door, having tucked the cookies in the crook of her arm. She reached through the door toward the top of her bureau and set the can down. After pushing her door open the rest of the way, she took her backpack off her shoulder and set it down on the floor next to her bed.

"Got any homework," her mom asked as she poked her head into Karla's room.

"Mom… Eh. Stop. Yes, I got homework, and I'm gonna do it tonight. Now leave me alone."

With that, she shut her bedroom door. Karla turned on her radio so she couldn't hear her mom anymore. She flopped down on her bed to listen to the music and to daydream about the cute guy in history.

Mrs. Centon stood staring at her daughter's bedroom door. Shut out once again. Didn't the girl know how hard she was trying to get better? It was so hard not to take that drink she so much wanted to have. She kept telling herself she'd to do this for Karla and her husband. Still sometimes after incidences like this when her daughter shut her out it made staying sober even harder.

There was no one for her to talk to and her family didn't seem to notice that she was trying to make things right. Depressed once again, Mrs. Centon went to sit alone in the living room, wishing the glass of water she was drinking happened to be something else.

## 8

KARLA HID IN HER ROOM FOR AS LONG AS SHE COULD. SHE FIDDLED with her cell phone passing the time away. She knew that as soon as she left the comfort of her room the questions would come again from her mom.

She kept her focus on learning the features of her phone. This made the time go by too quickly. Before she knew it, it was dinnertime.

"Karla, can you come set the table for dinner," her dad called from the kitchen. She'd never heard him come home and wondered how long he'd been there.

"Yeah, Dad, coming," Karla poked the button on her radio, shutting it off.

She left her phone sitting on her bureau, hooked up to its charger. She brought her empty soda can to the kitchen with her. She didn't have a trash bucket set up in her room yet. It was probably somewhere down in the basement with other miscellaneous items, which hadn't yet found a home.

Her dad was in the kitchen helping her mom with supper. A pot of spaghetti sauce simmered on the stove while her dad drained the spaghetti in the sink. Her mom was busy slicing a loaf of Italian bread.

It took her a couple of minutes to discover where her mom had hidden the plates. She found them in the cabinet above the breakfast nook. The search for the silverware was easier. Karla found them in the first drawer she opened.

She was not used to her dad being home for dinner. Usually, it was just her and her mom, and Karla would try to take her plate straight to her room. She was sure there would be none of that tonight, not with her dad there.

Karla set the table for dinner. She placed an empty glass beside each plate. Thoughts of Carol began entering her head. Thinking it'd be an opportune time to ask if she could go hang out with Carol since her dad was there tonight. He most likely would say yes.

She was nervous about asking her mom. Fearing her mom would say no, just for the sake of saying no. That was the way she was.

Karla waited for dinner to be almost over before she decided to bring Carol up in the conversation. She just hoped her dad would say she could hang out with her new friend.

The mall was so close by, and she wanted so badly to walk around it with no parental supervision. Maybe this was something her and Carol could do together while they hung out. Maybe walk around the mall or just around town. Karla would love to see what this place was all about.

Her mom broke the silence.

"Karla made a new friend in school today," beating Karla to the news of the day.

Karla twirled her spaghetti on the end of her fork. One strand seemed to elude her. She tipped her fork this way and that until finally it cooperated.

"Oh, sweetie, that's just great," her dad said as he shook more Parmesan onto his plate of spaghetti. His suit jacket hung on the chair behind him.

Karla twirled another fork full of spaghetti. The desire to ask her parents about hanging with Carol began to build up inside her until she couldn't stand it any longer.

She wondered if she should ask.

"Does she live near here," her dad asked after he washed a mouthful down with his drink. He scooped up another mouthful as he waited for her response.

"Just around the corner," Karla answered softly.

Her mom spoke up, "She said her name is Carol."

Obviously, her mom was excited about Karla's new friend. Karla was beginning to realize this. She didn't dare ask about hanging out with Carol while her mom was present, so she held the question back long enough for her mom to leave the room.

"Dad…I was wondering, can I go hang out with Carol this weekend?"

"I don't know. How much more unpacking do you've," her dad replied as he picked up his empty plate to carry into the kitchen.

She was afraid her mom would step in at any time and say no. Then it'd be the final decision at that stage. If she only could get her dad to say yes, right from the start.

Karla quickly finished her plate of food and followed him to the kitchen with her plate.

"I'm almost done unpacking. I should've it all done by tomorrow morning."

She rinsed her plate off in the sink and placed it in the dishwasher. She noticed her mom was still not in the kitchen; must be in the bathroom, she thought.

"Do you've any homework?" Her dad asked. He handed her more dishes to put in the dishwasher.

"Yeah, but I'm gonna do it tonight," Karla answered. She placed the glasses and coffee mugs on the top rack. The detergent, she poured into the holder and closed its lid.

"Please, Dad. Can I, please? You wanted me to make new friends, and I did. Can I please go hang out with Carol tomorrow," she pleaded.

Her mom jumped into the conversation, now that she was back in the kitchen.

"I don't know, Karla. You don't honestly know this girl that well yet. She could be one of those types of kids that are in trouble all the time."

"How can I get to know what she's like if I don't hang around with her," Karla pleaded. "I know how to stay out of trouble. If she does something we shouldn't do,

I'll come home immediately."

Karla shut the dishwasher and turned it on.

"Where are you and Carol going to be? I'm sure you're not going to stay around her house all day," her mom stated.

"I think she said something about going to the mall," Karla lied. She braced herself for her mom's big no. She was sure that'd be her mom's final answer.

Karla wanted to go to the mall badly, even if she'd to go there by herself, without Carol.

"The mall... That's where all kids get in trouble. They shoplift and get arrested. I don't think so. If you want to go to the mall, I'll take you there tomorrow night."

Her mom had the look in her eye. It was where her eyes looked a bit glazed over or slightly hazy. Karla tried to think back to how they looked when she'd gotten home from school. It was as if someone had actually been home inside her head earlier. This was so much different than they looked now.

Karla was beginning to feel sorry she'd even asked. She didn't feel like fighting tonight. She knew her mom would say no. Giving her dad one last pleading look, she braced herself for the final answer.

Her dad stepped in, "Come on, Laurette. She's almost seventeen. We've to start letting her learn from her own experiences. We can't go about protecting her for the rest of her life."

"All right... But if you get into any trouble I'll see to it you're grounded for months," her mom growled.

"Yes.

I promise I won't get into any trouble," she quickly hugged both her parents and retreated to her room. Hoping they wouldn't change their minds before tomorrow.

Karla was going to ask her dad about taking the wallpaper off her wall, but that could wait for another day.

She closed her bedroom door as soon as she entered the room, shutting her parents out of her life. Then she began her frantic search for Carol's phone number she'd given her earlier that day. Last time she'd seen it, she'd stuffed it somewhere inside her backpack.

All she could think about was how she was going to go to the mall without a parent chaperoning her. For the first time in her life, she'd have the chance not to feel like a geek.

Now all she'd to do was get a hold of Carol.

Where was the number?

# 9

KARLA DUMPED ALL HER BOOKS OUT ONTO HER BED. IT TOOK HER a few minutes of rummaging through all the stuff before she remembered where she'd stuffed the paper. She found the piece of yellow paper with Carol's phone number on it stuck in her math book. The paper torn almost in half, but it was still legible.

She then took a deep breath. Karla opened her cell phone and tapped out the number. The phone seemed to ring for more than five rings. She was about to hang up when someone answered the phone.

"Hi. Is Carol home?" Karla asked nervously.

"No, she's out right now."

"Okay... I'll call back later." Karla was relieved. She closed her phone and tossed it on her bed. Picking up her math book after deciding to do that first, and opened it to the homework assignment page. She hated math.

She struggled with her math homework for about half an hour, doing all but the last two equations. They were extra credit, anyway. Karla began to wonder what was on TV.

She looked around her room for her TV remote. It was lying on top of one of the unpacked boxes. She flipped through all the channels and found nothing she wanted to watch.

How can you've almost fifty channels on your TV and not be able to find anything you wanted to watch, especially on a Friday night?

Karla looked over at her alarm clock. She was surprised to see an hour had already gone by. She picked up her phone and gave Carol's number another try.

She punched out the numbers once again on the cell phone. This time on the third ring, someone answered the phone. It sounded like the same person who answered the last call.

"Hi, this is Karla. I called earlier. Is Carol home yet?" She wondered whether the individual on the other end of the phone happened to be Carol's mom. She feared they'd notice how shaky her voice seemed to sound.

"No... I'm sorry; she hasn't gotten back yet."

Karla was relieved but concerned at the same time. "All right...I'll try again later."

She wondered where Carol could be. It was getting late. She remembered she'd one more page to write on her report and decided to finish it, and then try Carol one last time. If she were not there this time, she'd have to try again tomorrow.

She worked on her report with her back to the clock so she couldn't watch the time. She'd put on her radio for background music since there was nothing on TV. When she finished the paper and put it into her notebook, it was almost 9:00.

After she had put her books and papers away, she gave Carol's number one last try. She punched out the numbers again. This time, she was a bit more relaxed. She figured she wouldn't be home yet anyway.

"Hi, this is Karla again. Is Carol home yet?" Karla asked after the fourth ring someone answered the phone.

"No, and it is late..."

Karla noticed how worried the person on the other end of the line sounded. "Do you know where she's?" She asked curiously.

"No. I don't."

"Could you let her know I called?" Karla requested. The worrisome sound of the receiver troubled her. "And that I'll try her again tomorrow."

The person on the other end of the line stated quickly, "Make sure you call her early in the morning, before nine or you may miss her again."

"All right, I'll, and thanks."

Karla wondered why Carol wasn't home. Could she have been out on a date? Maybe, but why didn't the person who answered the phone not know where she was?

Maybe Carol was sorry she'd given Karla her phone number and was there the whole time pretending not to be there. Maybe she actually didn't want to hang out with her after all. She grew more and more disappointed and sour by the minute just thinking about reasons why Carol wouldn't want to talk to her.

There wasn't anything else to do but either read a book or go to bed. Since she didn't feel like reading, she decided on crawling under her covers instead. Just as she was about to fall asleep, her cell phone began vibrating across her bureau, startling her.

Her heart skipped a beat as she jumped out of her bed to catch the phone before it slid off and onto the floor. She caught it at the last moment.

"Hello," Karla said after she opened her phone. This was the first time she'd received a cell phone call. The little flip phone appeared small in her hand. It might take a bit of time to get used to it.

The caller turned out not to be whom she'd expected it to be. It wasn't Carol. "Hey Karla, how was your first day?"

"I got the pictures you sent me today. Wow, your school is enormous. You weren't kidding, were you?"

It took Karla a moment to realize whom she was talking to.

"Sarah. I'm so glad you called..."

# 10

THE CLATTER OF SATURDAY MORNING BREAKFAST DISHES WOKE
Karla. She looked over at her alarm clock and saw it was already 9:00 in the morning.
She never slept in this late.

Her room was bright with the morning sun. She sat up in bed and took the remote for the TV and searched for something to watch. Finally, she settled for MTV.

Her room looked almost the way she wanted it to look. Karla had stayed up late
and had talked for nearly an hour to Sarah while she worked on her room. She only
had a couple of small boxes left to unpack, and these she'd stuffed into the bottom of
her closet. Most of her clothes that belonged on hangers were hung neatly. But, she
never bothered to close her closet door last night.

Karla could smell blueberry muffins cooking. They made her stomach growl. She
poked her head out her bedroom door.

"Are you making blueberry muffins for breakfast," she asked her mom.

Karla wandered out into the kitchen to have a better look.

"Yes. They'll be ready in another five minutes." Her mom flipped on the oven
light, showing Karla the big, puffy muffins browning in the oven.

She had plenty of time to get dressed while she waited and hurried back to her
room. The sound of a Monarch Pram video boomed from her TV. She quickly moved
to turn it down before her parents said something, surprised that her mom hadn't said
anything about the loud music yet.

Karla watched the video while she selected her outfit from her closet. She loved
her new closet. It was humongous, compared to the one she used to have. She could
hang her shoes and purses on the door. There were even little wire shelves to stack her
sweaters and things on.

When the video ended, Karla shut off her TV and began brushing her hair,
humming the last tune they'd played on the show. She tipped her head from one side
and then the other as she brushed her hair to the beat of the music.

She knew this tune would be stuck in her head for the rest of the day.

Karla slipped a clip into her hair to hold her hair back. It wasn't very long, but it was long enough to use the clip at the top of her head. She checked her appearance in the mirror and was satisfied with the results.

"Muffins are ready." Her mom called from the kitchen.

"Yup," Karla answered.

She tossed her brush on top of her bureau next to her cell phone. The sight of the phone reminded her that she was supposed to call Carol early this morning. It was now after 9 am. It was probably too late to call her.

So much for that idea, maybe she'd give her one last try later. She shrugged and decided to call after having that muffin. Since she hadn't made her bed, she closed her bedroom door to hid the fact. Her mother nagged her enough. She'd take care of it after she ate.

She noticed a paper plate with a muffin was waiting for her in the kitchen on the breakfast nook. "Muffins are good," Karla complimented her mom.

She could see her mom from where she sat. The breakfast nook was open below the cabinets. This allowed anyone sitting there to look out into the living room.

Her mom only raised a hand and waved an acknowledgment to her. She was busy reading. This didn't surprise Karla.

"Mom…I'm gonna go sit outside on the steps for a while," Karla announced when she was done eating. "I'm still waiting for Carol to call me back."

"Did you finish unpacking?"

"Yup, you can go check if you want."

"No, I believe you."

Good, Karla thought since she hadn't made her bed yet.

That was the first thing Karla did when she went back to her room. She quickly hurried to get it done doing a quick bedding fix to make it somewhat presentable. It mightn't meet her mom's expectations, but it met hers. Good enough, she thought.

The sun was out and it was already warm. It was probably going to be in the 80's today. She took a seat on the bottom step and was surprised to see how busy of a street they'd moved to. She could hear the sound of traffic from Main Street.

Someone's car alarm sounded somewhere nearby.

Karla watched the people walking and jogging up and down the street. There were a few kids from her school walking down the other side of the road. Could there be a park or a basketball court nearby?

The day was beginning to warm up quickly. Karla was glad she hadn't worn her blue hooded sweater like she originally had planned. She reached in her side pant pocket and felt for her cell phone. It was still there.

She took it out of her pocket to check it to see if she'd missed any calls. There was none. Still there was no return call from Carol. She put the phone back in her pocket.

A girl suddenly broke free from a group of teens across the street. Karla watched as she crossed the street and began jogging up her driveway. As she got closer, Karla realized it was Carol.

"Hey, Karla, my mom said you called me last night."

Carol sounded a bit out of breath.

Karla had stood up as soon as Carol began jogging up her short driveway.

"Yeah I did…

I called to let you know I could hang with you today. I just have to let my folks know where we're going to be."

"Oh. I was planning on going to the mall and maybe stop at the town field for a bit, 'cause Heath and Gerry have football practice later, and I was going to watch them."

"All right, hang on, I'll be right back, better yet, come on inside. You can meet my folks."

Karla brought Carol into the house. She was glad to see her dad was reading his newspaper. She hadn't been sure he was home. His car was not in the driveway.

Her mom was watching some cooking program on TV.

Most of the boxes were gone from the living room. The bookcase was assembled, and all the books had been neatly put away.

"Mom, Dad, this is Carol."

"Hi, Carol, it is nice to meet you."

Her dad looked up over the top of his newspaper.

"Karla says you live just down the street," her mom questioned.

"Yeah, I live at 292 Kemper Street. It is just around the corner from the library," Carol answered politely.

"Have you lived there long," her dad asked.

"Yeah, well, we've moved around town a couple of times. But I've lived in Brantwood all my life."

Carol smiled. She thought Karla's folks were kind of neat.

Karla hated the fact that her parents were beginning to throw twenty million questions at her new friend.

"Oh, so you must know your way around here real well," her mom asked.

"Um yeah, pretty much."

Carol looked bewildered by all the questions.

Karla butted in, "I'm gonna go with her to the mall if it is all right, and then we're gonna stop at the town field for a while. Is that okay?"

"Yes, but," her dad stated. "Be home before dark.

Her mom threw in, "And stay out of trouble."

"Thanks."

Karla hoped the question time was over for now. She began to move toward the door. Turning, she checked to see if Carol was following her.

"Bye – It was nice meeting you," Carol said politely.

Karla caught Carol by her sleeve.

She tried not to look too obvious to her parents in her eagerness to leave.

She said quietly to Carol, "Come on, let's go before they change their minds."

"Why? Your folks seem pretty nice," Carol smiled.

Karla led Carol out the door.

"My mom can be a witch. My dad, yeah, he can be sweet at times. He can even be cool at times, too. But he does have his moments."

The traffic got thicker. They'd to stop and wait before crossing the street. Walking silently, they made their way to the corner of Main Street.

Carol stopped before the entrance to the small convenience store.

"Karla, I'm gonna get a drink, you want one?"

"I didn't bring any money with me," Karla responded.

She wished she had, though. She would've liked to have been able to get herself another outfit, or maybe a Cd or something.

"That's okay. You stay here, I'll be right back," Carol called over her shoulder.

Karla watched while Carol entered the store and headed toward the back, out of sight. The store may have been small, but there were a lot of customers inside, from what she could see from where she stood.

She turned toward the traffic and began watching the people and cars. She was amused by the sight of a dog trying to cross a crosswalk by itself. Its owner appeared to be nowhere in sight.

Carol spooked Karla with her sudden appearance. She pulled a candy bar out of one pocket of her hoodie and handed it to Karla.

"You can have half. Go ahead, open it." Carol then produced a can of soda from the other pocket of her hoodie.

"Wow, that was quick. Wasn't there a big line? Did you cut in line or something?"

"I know the owner." Carol popped the top on her soda and took her share of the candy bar.

"Oh. Right, whatever works, I guess."

Karla took a bite of the candy bar and began following Carol along the sidewalk. Many small shops lined the street. They were all facing a large town common with several park benches. She followed Carol for what seemed like a half an hour.

"How far to the mall?"

"We're Almost there."

Carol drained the last of her soda. She flipped the can into a trash bin as they passed by.

"Cool…"

She'd never met such a fast walker. Karla wondered why they had to walk so fast. She was having trouble keeping up with her. They walked for another two blocks, and then Karla saw the sign.

"I' haven't been here in months."

Carol slowed up a bit. "Good. I can still plan on having some fun by showing you around."

The mall grew before Karla's eyes. She thought it must've been about a mile long. Her eyes scanned the signs of store names mounted above each of the individual stores. She was thrilled to see her favorite store was still part of this mall.

"Can we go into Abercrombie? I want to check out their outfits," she asked Carol as she spied the store sign.

Karla followed Carol across the busy parking lot. Drivers appeared to fight over some of the spots. She remembered what it was like when her Dad tried to park at this mall last Christmas. It was horrible.

Carol led Karla straight to the main entrance of the mall. She was amazed by the flood of people. She never realized how busy this place could be even when it wasn't near the holidays.

"I know where the Abercrombie store is," Carol stated.

Carol picked up the pace again; making Karla wondered why she'd to walk so fast. She'd to sidestep around people so she could keep up with her in the thick crowd. The task was proving to be difficult. She almost had to push her way through the people to keep up with her.

Carol stopped quickly, and Karla almost walked into her. "Here it is."

Karla followed Carol into the store. She heard the door chime when she stepped onto the entrance carpet. Carol immediately began checking out some tops neatly folded on a square table.

"Hey, I like this one." Carol held up the top in front of herself for Karla to see.

"Ah, yeah, that one is really nice," Karla agreed.

"I've got to try it on." Carol took the top to the dressing room, along with a pair of pants and a couple of other outfits.

Karla followed Carol. She grabbed a few outfits to try on too, even though she didn't bring any money to buy them. She could at least see how they'd look on her. If she liked them, maybe she could come back later and buy them.

She showed the outfits she wanted to try on in the dressing room to the store clerk. The clerk gave them each a tag with some items they had with them.

Karla took the booth next to Carol's.

She put the first outfit on. The pants seemed to be a little tight around her waist. While the top was just a bit lower cut than what she was used to. After checking it out in the mirror, she stepped out of the booth.

"What do you think?" She wanted Carol's opinion.

Carol stepped out of her booth after putting on the top she'd wanted to try on. "Oh, that does look beautiful on you. How 'bout mine? You like?"

She turned around in front of the mirror, trying to see what it looked like in the back.

"Yeah," Karla approved. She held up the price tag for Carol to see. "Too bad it's so expensive."

"Eh, that never stops me," Carol stated. She looked one more time in the mirror, admiring the top. Her fingers quickly found the price tag and snapped it off.

"What're you doing?" Karla asked, surprised by Carol's actions.

"Nothing," Carol looked out the fitting room door and saw Heath and Gerry. She pointed Heath out to Karla. "Hey, look, there is Heath. Go let him know I'll be right out."

"Okay," Karla stepped back into her booth to change. She didn't finish trying on all her outfits. It didn't matter anymore. All she wanted to do was get out of there fast after she saw what Carol had done with the price tag.

Nervous jitters grew in the pit of her stomach as she stepped out of her booth and checked in Carol's. It was empty. The jitters got worse.

She stopped to drop off the number tag and the outfits. Carol was nowhere to be seen. Karla saw Heath standing a few yards from the entrance of the store. Fearing she'd be watched because of what Carol had just done, she walked as calmly as she could. The door chime announced Karla's departure making her jump just a little bit. She hoped no one saw how tense she was.

"Heath, Carol said she'll be right out."

"Is she getting another outfit?" Heath asked.

"Um...I'm not sure...She said she'll be out in a minute."

Karla wasn't sure what Carol was really doing. She didn't see her standing in line, and she was taking what seemed like a long time.

"Here she comes," Heath announced. He immediately turned away and started walking away from the store.

"Hey, Heath," Carol called as she quickly became in step with Heath.

"Karla, keep walking until I say we can stop," she said as she grabbed Karla by the sleeve and pulled her along with them.

"Huh?" Carol's sudden appearance stunned Karla.

"Just do as she says," Heath interjected over his shoulder.

"Oh, right." Karla moved up beside Carol. She almost had to jog to keep up with them.

"Hey, Carol, Heath, where are you guys headed," Gerry asked. He suddenly appeared beside Heath.

"Gerry. Um, we're on our way to the food court. You wanna join us," Carol smiled. She looked over at Karla and winked at her.

"Sure...You going to practice today? It's at one," Gerry asked. He glanced at Heath and Carol. He smiled when his eyes locked onto Karla's.

"Yeah, us girls need to get something to eat first."

Carol turned to Karla, "What do you want, Karla?"

"Oh, I don't know. I think I'll be all set."

Karla's heart was fluttering at the unexpected appearance of Gerry. This was added to the butterfly flutters of what she thought had taken place back in the store.

Her thoughts raced, now that she knew his name. She couldn't believe he was here, the cute guy from history. Maybe, just maybe, Carol would help fix her up with him. She knew the possibility was there since Carol had winked at her just a few moments ago when Gerry had appeared.

"She wants a burger," Carol barked at the boys. "You want cheese on that? Yeah...I think she wants cheese on that. Oh, and diet sodas for both of us. Thanks, guys."

Karla overcame her sudden shock of seeing Gerry and finally spoke up. "Carol...I didn't want anything."

"Well, you got to eat. Let the guys get it. Let's sit over here."

She led Karla to a table in the middle of the food court. Taking the sleeve of her hoodie, she wiped off the table.

"Did I see you take that outfit back there?" Karla was miffed by Carol's apparent behavior.

"No… you must've been seeing things." Carol giggled.

Karla watched Carol open her bag, showing the outfit inside. "Oh my God… Carol. How could you," Karla aspirated.

"Easy. I do it all the time. You should try it sometime. It's fun," Carol smiled.

"Fun till you get caught. Here is your kibble, ladies." Heath joked as he placed a tray in front of Carol.

"So what did you get this time," Gerry added, "I hope you tried it on first."

Karla accepted the food quietly. She watched and listened to the conversation unfolding in front of her.

Gerry took the seat across from her. He made her jittery by sitting so close. Her eyes kept drifting to his face, she was consciously staring at him as he ate.

"You should've seen the last outfit she took. She would've had to lose fifty pounds to fit into it," Gerry teased Carol. "Were you smokin' crack that day?

Carol stuck out her tongue at Gerry.

"No, Gerry. I got that outfit for Cassie. She was wearing it yesterday. Didn't you see it?"

"Hell, Carol, you don't even like Cassie. You only gave it to her 'cause it don't fit you," Heath teased her.

"Man, that'd've been a bummer if you'd gotten caught stealing an outfit that didn't even fit you," Gerry snickered as he took a swallow of his soda.

"Ha. See if I get you anything," Carol fought back.

Gerry glanced at his watch, "Heath, we got to get to practice."

He gathered up his lunch to take with him.

"See you girls later?"

Heath gave Carol a quick kiss after piling his trash onto Carol's tray.

"Yeah…We'll be there in a bit."

Carol finished the last bite of her burger.

Gerry stopped and smiled at Karla.

"Karla, you gonna eat those fries?"

"No, you can have them." Karla handed them to him. His fingers touched hers briefly making her heart go tingly.

"Thanks," Gerry smiled, taking a french fry from the bag, he bit down on it. Making some clicking sound with his mouth, he turned to leave with Heath.

# 11

KARLA WAS NOT SURE WHAT THEY'D BE DOING NEXT. SHE WAITED for some sort of clue to come from Carol. She watched her stand, taking her tray to the trash, so Karla mimicked her actions. She wanted to fit in so badly with Carol and her other friends that she'd do just about anything to keep from acting like some sort of outsider.

They departed in the opposite direction from the way the boys had gone. Karla followed Carol through the mall.

When they found the entrance, Karla pushed through the doors behind Carol. She was so glad to be out of there. She'd this nagging fear ever since they'd left the food court, fearing the mall security would come running after them at any given moment.

Her phone startled her when it began to vibrate and sound in her pocket. Karla opened it up and saw the phone number on the caller ID.

"Oh, great," Karla exclaimed.

"What's wrong," Carol stopped and asked.

"It's my mom," Karla explained.

She spoke into the phone, "Hey, Mom."

"Karla, are you going to be much longer?"

"I don't know... Why?"

"I just spoke with Sarah's mom. She mentioned how much Sarah wanted to spend the rest of the weekend with you, so I invited her over."

"Really...," Karla asked while she glanced at Carol.

"She's on her way over right now."

"What about Jody? Is she coming, too?"

"Sarah mentioned something about Jody. I told her she was invited, too."

"Awesome. When'll they be here?"

"Soon…"

"Okay… I'll be home soon, then. Thanks, Mom." Karla closed her phone and stuffed it back into her pocket. "I got to head back now."

"You're not going to watch practice," Carol asked, she sounded surprised.

"No, maybe next time…I got to go…"

"I'll see you in school on Monday, then."

" …later then."

She waved to Carol and then broke into a jog, she was anxious to get home. The day's events were still troubling her. She couldn't believe that she'd possibly witnessed Carol stealing something from the store. What would her friends say if she told them about it?

Karla thought about this some more.

They probably would tell her that Carol was trouble. But what was Karla supposed to do? She was in a new school and didn't know a soul. No one else had tried to become friends with her yet. The way they looked at her made her feel like a foreigner or something. She hated it when people stared at her.

But as Karla got closer to home she wasn't so anxious about Carol. She seemed to want to be friends with her, and her and her friends seemed pretty cool to hang with. They just made her a little bit nervous to be around them. Their behaviors seemed so strange to her. She just couldn't understand why she'd taken the outfit, and couldn't get it out of her head.

She was so glad they didn't get caught. Her mom would've killed her.

# 12

SHE TIDIED UP HER BED AS SOON AS SHE GOT HOME. NOW, SHE
knelt on the bed while she peered out her window, waiting for her friends to arrive.
Karla still didn't see Sarah's car yet, she'd been waiting for almost an hour. They'd
called to let her know that they were on their way.

She put on a Hip Hop CD and adjusted the volume so her folks wouldn't complain. Her and her friends loved Terry Moniat, she was the hottest on the charts right
now. Many times they made wishful plans of attending one of her concerts.

Karla kept checking out the window and moving about her room, tidying it up
more and more. She moved her school books. The piece of paper with Carol's number on it fell out of her math book when she stuffed the books underneath the bed.
She didn't want to lose the number in case she wanted to call Carol again.

She pondered for a moment, letting her eyes scan the room for the perfect place
to stash the number. Her eyes settled on her purse hanging from her desk chair. She
stuffed the paper into one of its side pockets.

A car pulled up in the driveway, beeping its horn. Karla looked out the window
again. She saw Sarah and Jody climb out of the car, swinging their bags over their
shoulders. Excited, Karla ran to the front door.

Sarah wore another one of her bright-colored t-shirts. This one was a bright red
with a big old frog pictured on the front of it. Her hair was braided and pinned up
against the back of her head. Flip flops accompanied her skinny jeans.

Jody, being slightly overweight would never be found dead or alive wearing
skinny jeans. She preferred lightweight active wear pants and oversized shirts. Hoping
the shirts would hide some of her misshapen form. She also wore flip-flops, but Karla
could see the sneakers tied to the loop of her backpack.

Karla remembered how Jody tried to diet and knew she couldn't hold fault
against her weight problem. Diets just never worked out well for her.

Even Sarah and Karla tried to do the diet thing with Jody to help support her. Of course, the diet worked well for Sarah. She was thin to begin with so it didn't take much for her to lose even more weight.

Karla lost about four pounds on the diet but gained it all back within a matter of months.

But Jody, though, she gained an additional ten pounds by the end of their dieting episode. What a bummer it'd been for her. She never tried to diet ever again.

Mrs. Centon was already at the door, letting Sarah and Jody in before Karla got to the living room.

"Sarah, Jody, I'm so glad to see you. Karla, your friends are here."

"Coming," Karla answered from the kitchen. "Sarah, Jody. Awesome! You made it." Karla hugged her friends. This was the longest she'd ever been away from them. "Bring your stuff to my room."

She saw their eyes gaze around the room.

"I'll give you a tour afterward."

"Cool house," Sarah complimented.

"This is awesome, Karla," Jody agreed.

"Jody, you got your hair cut again. I like it," Mrs. Centon pointed out.

"Oh thanks, Mrs. Centon. I'd it done yesterday. The humidity was making it curl too much, and the friezes were starting to drive me nuts. I wanted to dye it to a different color, but my mom wouldn't let me. I hate having black hair. It is so."

Mrs. Centon said, "There is nothing wrong with your hair color. I rather like it the way it is."

Karla grabbed Jody by the arm and dragged her and Sarah to her room. She pointed out where the bathroom was as they walked down the hallway to her room, explaining to them how her parents' room was at the end of the hall.

"She's got a pool, too," Sarah boasted while placing her things on the bedroom floor, "We got to go check it out. She said it's out back."

"We don't have any water in it yet. Dad is getting it ready for winter," Karla replied as she brought her friends outdoors to see the pool and the backyard.

Karla had discovered a large tree in the back corner of the yard the other day. That was the day she'd seen the pool for the first time. They sat under it and discussed the week's events at school. Karla so missed her old school, even the kids she'd never gotten along with.

A delicious odor came from the open window of the house. "Hey, let's go in now. I think my Mom is making cookies."

In the kitchen, Karla's mom was putting washed dishes away. A bowl of cookie dough sat on the counter. The oven light was on exposing the baking sheet of cookies.

"Hey, Mom, you're making cookies?"

"Yup, thought you girls would like some," Mrs. Centon smiled.

"Cool. Chocolate chip. Thanks, Mrs. Centon."

Jody snatched a finger of dough from the bowl.

"I can't wait for the pool parties this summer," Sarah said excitedly to Karla's Mom.

"This is gonna be so awesome, to come over to Karla's to swim and party. If only Debbie and her scum friends could see us now," Jody agreed while licking the last of the dough from her fingers.

Karla took a seat at the breakfast nook with Jody and Sarah and listened while they filled Mrs. Centon in about the people who moved into their old house. They'd built a small shed in the backyard for a pony. Karla frowned while remembering how much she'd wanted a horse a few years ago. Her parents had told her, "No pony."

"Hey, let's go in my room and listen to music, watch movies, or something," Karla suggested to her friends.

Mrs. Centon held out a plate of cookies. "Karla, here take this plate of cookies with you." They were still warm.

"Thanks, Mom," Karla replied as she happily accepted the plate of cookies.

"Jody, can you grab three sodas from the fridge?" Mrs. Centon took the drinks from the refrigerator. Sarah took one and Jody took the other two. They followed Karla to her room leaving Mrs. Centon alone in the kitchen.

They piled into Karla's bedroom and took seats on the floor while Karla closed the bedroom door behind them, giving them added privacy from her parents.

Her dad hadn't stripped the walls like he'd promised her he'd. She could just hear the comments her friends would be saying about her wallpaper. About how ugly it was.

"So what's your week been like at your new school," Sarah asked Karla.

"Actually, it seems to be going well. I met this girl, Carol; she lives a couple of streets over. She wants me to try out for volleyball."

"You, play volleyball? Ha. That, I got to see," Jody joked. She handed Karla her soda and took a cookie from the plate.

"Why volleyball, you never liked volleyball before," Sarah asked. A jeering smile crossed her face making Karla feel defensive.

"I don't know; I guess, 'cause Carol plays volleyball, she only asked me. I don't think I'm gonna do it anyway. As you said, I don't like volleyball," Karla answered. She bit into the cookie, turned the TV on, and shut off the stereo. Flipping through the DVD's in a box on her floor, she found one she knew her friends would like.

"Well, it's all good that you're making new friends. Just don't forget about us." Jody responded.

"You know I'll never forget about either of you," Karla turned on the DVD player and slipped the disk into the drive.

"Just checking," Jody said as she cracked open her soda can.

"Hey, do you think we can go to the mall tomorrow," Sarah asked.

"I don't know."

"Your mom is really nice tonight," Sarah picked up the DVD jacket. She flipped it over to glance at the back of it.

"I guess she does have her moments," Karla picked up her remote and began fast-forwarding past the movie previews.

A rap sounded at the door. The door knob turned and opened. Karla's mom's head poked around the door. "Girls, I hate to bother you, but can you stay up no later than 1:00. Stan has to go to work tomorrow, and we don't want to keep him up all night."

Karla replied an agreement and quickly shooed her Mom away.

Sarah handed the movie jacket over to Jody as Karla took a seat on the floor between them. She placed the plate of cookies on the floor in front of her and was surprised no one had said anything about the ugly wallpaper. It was just as well, she thought.

"Oh, I haven't seen that one," Jody stated. She flipped the jacket over to read the back.

For the next few hours, Karla, Sarah, and Jody watched the movie. Every once in a while they'd chat about what was going on in the gossip news at Medham High.

Then Karla would tell them a little bit about her new classes and teachers. She purposely left out any information about Carol. She was still not sure about telling them about her day at the mall.

But then again, she wasn't even sure if Carol had actually stolen that outfit after all. It may have been just her imagination.

Forget about Carol, she told herself. Her real friends were here, and that should be all that mattered.

# 13

KARLA WOKE WITH THE SUN BLARING IN HER EYES. SHE ROLLED over in her bed to see her friends sound asleep on the floor, wrapped in blankets. Her TV displayed a screen filled with white noise. They must've fallen asleep while watching the movie.

Sarah opened her eyes and looked up at Karla.

"You awake," she asked groggily.

"Yeah...Is Jody still asleep?"

Karla pushed herself up onto her elbow. She was trying to see if she could see any movement coming from Jody.

Sarah pulled herself with her blankets closer to Jody and poked her in the side.

"You awake?"

"Cut the crap." Jody snarled.

Karla and Sarah giggled.

"You're not much of a morning person, are you?"

Karla sat up and scooted to the edge of her bed.

"At least I watched most of the movie. You guys were out not long after it started. Too bad too, it was a real good movie."

Jody sat up. Her blankets were in a pile about her waist.

"Mom made blueberry muffins yesterday, want some?"

Karla rifled through her dresser drawer for an outfit to wear. She found one to her liking and tossed it onto her bed.

"...that sounds good."

Jody pushed her blankets into a pile in an empty corner of the room. She grabbed her bag and pulled out her clothes, changing into them.

"Yeah, I'll have some."

Sarah picked up her bag and carried it into the bathroom.

When Sarah returned back to the room, her hair was pinned up on the back of her head again. This time she donned a bright purple T-shirt with a bright yellow star on the front of it. Karla thought it looked hideous, but she knew Sarah loved this shirt.

Jody wore an oversized blue top which hung way past her waistline. Her black pants matched the flip flops she was wearing. Karla smiled to herself. Jody was her friend; she was just big boned.

Karla led her friends to the kitchen. Sarah and Jody each took a seat at the breakfast nook. Mrs. Centon was in the living room reading a book.

"Mom, are there any muffins left?"

Karla opened the fridge to take out a small carton of juice.

"I put them in the refrigerator…Would you like me to heat them up for you?"

Mrs. Centon put her book down and came into the kitchen. She opened the fridge, pulling a plate of muffins out and set it down on the counter before the girls.

"No…they're good the way they are," Sarah replied.

Mrs. Centon gave each of them a napkin for their muffins. Karla took the seat between her two friends. The muffins were good, even though they were cold and a day old.

"What're you girls planning on doing today," asked Mrs. Centon while she stood in front of the breakfast nook, sipping her coffee.

"Mom, is it okay with you, that we walk to the mall?"

"I guess. Just make sure you stick together."

Mrs. Centon took another sip of her coffee. She really wished it was something else even if it was early in the day. She couldn't remember exactly how long it'd been since she'd had her last drink. Maybe she'd made it a week, she wasn't certain. She craved its relaxing effect it had on her. Kids always had the tendency to make her uptight. They never listened to a word she said. Just like Karla, and she hated it when her daughter rolled her eyes at her, as she was doing now.

"So, you're older now, and at the age when girls have no problem sticking together. Well, just make sure you take your cell phone with you, just in case I've to get a hold of you for some reason."

Karla reached into her pocket to display her phone.

"Oh. I see that's not an issue, either."

Karla didn't wait for her mom to change her mind. She wrapped her muffin up in her napkin and gulped down her juice with Sarah and Jody following her lead, and they hurried to the door before she could change her mind.

"…you girls be careful, then. Watch out for traffic, and stay out of the alleyways and be home by 4:00 for supper," Karla's Mom called after them as they exited out the door.

They'd escaped into the street elated by the fact that the three of them were well on their way to the mall with no embarrassing parent accompanying them.

# 14

SARAH SAID, "I THINK YOUR MOM IS TRYING," AS THEY WALKED
from the house to the driveway.

"I know. I just wish she wasn't so overprotective. It drives me nuts," Karla complained.

She glanced over her shoulder to see if her mom was standing in the doorway watching her, and was relieved to see her gone from sight.

"How far is the mall from here," Jody asked. She started at the sound of squealing tires. This was a sort of noise one usually didn't hear in their neck of the woods. It made her look in the direction of the squeal, expecting to see a couple of cars crashing into one another.

A blue sports car pulled up quick to the sidewalk across the street. Karla spotted Carol walking toward them, but she was on the other side of the road. Stopping fast, Karla looked to see if any cars were coming. Now was her time to introduce Carol to her best friends.

"Oh, just another block, hey, that's Carol." Karla pointed out her new friend to Sarah and Jody. "She goes to my school. She's the one who wanted me to try out for volleyball. Come on, let's go say hi. I'll introduce you to her." Karla stepped off the sidewalk to cross the street. She hesitated, waiting for her friends to catch up.

"Karla, I don't know…Who are the dudes with her?" Jody asked.

Karla turned back to see if Carol was looking her way yet. She still was only one step off the sidewalk. Hearing an approaching car, she nervously stepped back onto the sidewalk with her friends.

"Oh…I've never met them." Karla watched while Carol climbed into the strange car. She wasn't sure of what to tell her friends about Carol. The shoplifting incident in the mall still sat in the back of her mind. She was not sure Jody would approve of her new friend. "Rats, we missed her. I wonder where she's headed. I guess we'll have to catch up with her another time."

Karla was relieved to put off introducing her old friends to her new friend. She wanted to get to know Carol a bit more before she introduced them all to each other. She refused to consider this anymore and continued leading her friends to the mall. Maybe she'd do it next time. She'd see…

There seemed to be even more traffic today than Karla remembered seeing yesterday. She began to walk faster as the mall grew larger, excited to bring her friends along without having parental supervision. She never thought this day would come.

"Cool…the movie theater is next to the mall."

Sarah pointed to the movie theater outside the mall parking lot.

"Let's see what's playing," Jody said as she turned to follow Sarah to the theater.

"Maybe we can hit the food court afterward. I'm starving, that muffin just didn't do the trick for me," suggested Karla.

"Look. 'To the Max' is playing. I really want to see that," said Jody as she pointed at the movie poster.

Sarah stated, "Well then, let's go get something to eat, and afterward go to the matinee. It's cheaper."

"Awesome. I didn't know this movie was playing. Did everyone bring enough money to get in," asked Karla?

"Yeah… I got enough," Jody said. "I just won't buy that new outfit I was gonna get."

"I can lend you some Jody if you need it," Sarah offered.

"Na I'll be all right," replied Jody. "I can get it some other time."

Karla almost let it slip. She almost told them she'd been here the day before with Carol. They stopped at the mall map center to locate the food court. Karla pretended to study the map. She hoped they wouldn't be going anywhere near Abercrombie, she feared she'd be recognized from the day before when she'd been there with Carol.

She'd die if she were accused of stealing from the store in front of her friends, even if she hadn't had anything to do with what Carol had taken. She was still guilty about the whole thing.

The store loomed off to their right. She'd never been so happy before to have been able to avoid Abercrombie. She made certain to keep her eyes from looking in its direction, lest her friends mistake her casual glance at the store to be a need to enter it to window shop. That could prove to be disastrous.

# 15

THE MALL WAS PACKED. KARLA STOPPED SHORT. SHE ALMOST
walked into a young mother pushing a stroller who happened to stop suddenly to pick
up a lost bottle.

The pet shop window caught her attention. She waved to Sarah and Jody to
come look in the Shop's window with her.

"Ah... Look, kitties. Aren't they cute? I wish my folks would let me get one,"
groaned Karla.

"Hey there, cutie...," Sarah waved at a kitten, "Oh, look ... That one seems like a
runt. Isn't it cute?" Sarah pointed to the fluffy white kitten.

Karla spotted Gerry across the way. He was walking with his friends as they went
past the pet store and came to stop at the shop across from the pet store. It was an
electronics shop.

She saw him laughing at something Heath had just said. Her throat suddenly
tightened, and butterflies flopped around in her stomach.

"Yup," Karla grabbed Sarah by the arm. She looked behind her to see if Jody
was following. Satisfied with the spot they now stood in, she allowed her eyes to rest
on Gerry again. They were now out of direct line of sight and had to peer over a tall
planter with a fake palm tree.

"Look, but don't stare," Karla instructed her friends, "That's the guy I was telling
you about."

She pointed out Gerry to Jody and Sarah.

"Isn't he cute? Oh God, here he comes," she giggled nervously, "Let's go in here
and look at the rest of the animals."

She latched onto Sarah's arm and dragged her into the pet store.

"He might look good – to you, but he looks kind of like a jerk to me." Sarah
stopped just inside the shop and looked in Gerry's direction. She then turned back to
admire the rabbits in the cage before her so it wouldn't appear to him or his friends
that she was apparently watching him.

"I heard at lunch the other day that he's the Football Captain. He just looks rough 'cause he has to," Karla said defensively.

"I don't know…" Jody said. "He kind of gives me the willies too. My folks taught me to trust my instincts about people, and I've to say he actually gives me the willies.

"Looks don't always show what a person is like on the inside."

"You're just saying that. How 'bout when you went out with Dave last year," Karla demanded.

"Dave was a mistake, and I learned from that," Jody retorted.

"Don't get her wrong; she still talks to Dave. They just don't see each other anymore," Sarah blurted. She was afraid to choose sides between her two friends. So she always tried to keep to the middle ground.

Karla sneered, "You still talk to that jerk, and you talk about me?"

"Yeah…I talk to him…. Just talk…We aren't even really friends anymore," Jody defended.

"He went out with Carrie last month, and she said he tried to rape her, too," Sarah said as she picked up a dog toy and began to squeak it.

"Someone needs to turn him into the police," Karla replied as she too took a toy. It was a cat toy with little bells. After giving it a shake, she put it back on the shelf.

"The problem is that it is our word against his, and we've no way of proving any of it." Jody picked up a book on how to train dogs. She slowly flipped through the pages.

"There has to be some way to stop him," demanded Karla.

"Yeah….When she finally gets a new boyfriend who isn't a wimp. She'll get him to beat the crap out of him," Sarah giggled.

"No…" Jody chuckled, "I'll just warn any girl that decides to go out with him to be on guard against him…just in case he tries anything with them."

"Someday, just warning the girl isn't gonna be enough," Karla complained. "He's gonna hurt someone, someday, and you're gonna wish you'd stepped forward and said something to the authorities."

"Well, if that day comes, then I'll step forward and tell the authorities. Until then, I just keep my distance from him," Jody retorted.

Karla glanced out the shop door. "Hey, he's gone now. Let's get something to eat and then go see our movie."

As they walked to the food court, Karla thought back to the end of their school year. Back when Jody went out on her very first date with a guy she'd met while picking up a few things for her mom at the store. His name was Dave.

At first Dave seemed to be a kind of nice guy. He and Jody would take walks around her neighborhood or just stop by for quick visits.

He even met her parents before asking her out on the date. They even seemed to like him.

Dave had dinner and a movie planned for their date. At least that's what he'd told Jody.

In fact, Jody never really suspected anything was off with him even when they pulled up in front of his place and he let her know they were at their destination. She just thought he'd to run inside to get something, assuming they then would be right back out and on their way to the restaurant.

She never even noticed him locking the door behind him.

The meal was already prepared and set up romantically on the table with roses in a vase and nice place settings. Almost like a professional designer had set the room up for the occasion.

All went well with the meal and lots of small talk. Jody still didn't suspect anything.

After they had eaten, he took their empty plates to the kitchen and told Jody to make herself comfortable in the living room.

It was decorated with fine furniture. It was almost too fine and made Jody wonder what Dave did for work to be able to pay for such things for a guy his age.

When he was done in the kitchen, which didn't take him long to do, he came into the living room holding a video camera. Jody asked him what he planned on doing with it and she wanted to know when, where and what movie they were going to go see.

That was when he informed her that they weren't going to see a movie but were going to make the movie instead. Jody was horrified...

She never told her friends the rest of the details to the evening, nor how she'd escaped him. They only knew that she had and that she was so glad her dad had made her take that karate class last year. Even though she'd never gotten past the green belt, all that she'd learned may have saved her life.

Apparently she must've kicked his ass and kicked it good. Why else would she still talk to him?

At the food court, Karla sat across from Jody and thought more about the whole incident. All she could do was admire Jody for having sheer guts. That's what Jody had – guts and more guts.

# 16

THE ACTION PACKED MOVIE WAS ONE OF THE LONGEST MOVIES THE girls had been to. But, the leading actor was awfully handsome, flamboyant, and such a smooth talker. And, to top it off, the movie was also funny at times. So funny, that Karla choked on her soda during one moment in the movie. Her nose still burned.

"That movie was great," Sarah slung her purse strap over her shoulder.

"Yeah...Want the rest of my popcorn?"

Jody offered the popcorn container to Karla.

"Na...you can chuck it."

Karla nodded toward the closest trash bin. She glanced out the window. It was beginning to get dark out. Opening her cell phone, she checked the time. She couldn't believe it was already that late. The movie was long, but she didn't think it was that long.

"Oh, look at the time...We better get back, or Mom will ground me for sure."

"Why don't you call her and let her know the movie just got out," Sarah suggested.

"Oh, yeah...I guess I can do that."

Karla flipped the phone back open. She imagined her mom yelling at her over the phone in front of her friends. Nervously, she punched in the number. Two rings, then her mom answered the phone.

"Mom, the movie just got out. We're heading home now," Karla winced, bracing for the coming lecture.

"Karla, I'm glad you used your head and called," her mom praised.

"Oh." Karla didn't know what to say. Stunned, she waited for her mom to speak.

"Well ...You'll have to heat up your meals when you get home because we went ahead and ate without you."

"...We'll be home soon," Karla knew her voice shook. She hoped none of her friends noticed how she sounded. Her mom's response surprised her, she snapped her phone closed. "Wow, she didn't even sound angry..."

"Cool," Jody remarked. "Let's go… it's starting to get dark out." She led the way out of the theater.

The parking lot was full of cars. The next showing would be starting in fifteen minutes. Karla couldn't believe how many people there was at the movie theater. They must all have been there waiting to see the movie the girls had just gone to see. Apparently it was a lot more popular than she'd thought.

It'd been that good. She even bet it'd get an award this year, for best-supporting actor. Or, at least she hoped.

Karla walked between her two friends. Walking in silence, she really hated to see her friends go. Her mood dulled while the street lights came on lighting their way home. A car passed them like the one she saw Carol climb into. She began to think about Carol, wondering if she was home yet. Maybe she'd call her later, after Sarah and Jody went home.

"I wish you guys could stay another night," Karla blurted out, trying to break the silence. The silence had an eerie feel to it and it troubled her.

"Yeah…," Sarah agreed. "Too bad we got school tomorrow, or I'd ask otherwise." She reached out to push the stop light button. Cars began to line up in front of the crosswalk.

"And; I've to work tomorrow," Jody replied as she looked down the street, watching the traffic.

"I guess I should start looking for a job," Karla said as the crosswalk light changed to green, allowing her to step off the curb. "Maybe I can get one somewhere in the mall."

"Then we'd never have any time to spend together," Jody complained. She turned around, walking backward in front of Karla.

"I'm getting my license soon," Sarah said, skipping over a crack in the sidewalk. "We could hang out on weekend nights. The movies are open late."

"I don't know if my folks would let me stay out late…," Karla said, "You know how they are."

"You never know until you ask," Sarah advised.

The driveway appeared small in the darkness. An outside light on the edge of the driveway beckoned their way to the door.

"I guess we'll see," Karla reluctantly opened the door and announced, "Mom, we're home."

"Okay, go get washed up, and I'll heat this up for you girls." The microwave beeped. Her mom headed into the kitchen to finish heating up the meals.

Karla noticed her mom seemed angry. She was surprised to see that she was heating up their meal since she did say they'd have to heat it up themselves, over the phone.

They quickly washed up and took their places at the dinner table. Mrs. Centon served them leftover frozen pizza. It was a little tough and chewy from the microwave, but it was still edible.

Mrs. Centon took a place at the table. She cradled some sort of drink in a glass of ice, between the palms of her hands. Karla couldn't tell what kind it was, but she did know it was not soda. She wondered how much of that stuff her mom would drink before going to bed tonight. Giving it some thought, she couldn't remember how long it'd been since she'd seen one of those drinks in her mom's hands.

Karla did make one other note. Her dad's car was not in the driveway. She didn't remember him saying he'd to go out tonight.

"So, what did you girls do today, anyway," Mrs. Centon asked.

Karla raised an eyebrow and she stated defensively, "We went to the mall and the movies, Mom, remember."

"I know that. I just wanted to know what you did while you were there."

Karla began to feel nervous. She didn't know where these questions were leading. Was her mom going to revert to her old self before Sarah and Jody left? And where was her dad, why was he not here?

"We just walked around the mall and watched a movie."

Jody jumped in to rescue Karla, "Yeah and we stopped at the pet shop. They have the cutest little kittens, fluffy white ones."

"And we saw the movie, "To the Max"; it's got John Mosston in it. He's so good. I see all of his movies whenever I can," Sarah added.

Mrs. Centon took another sip of her drink. "I'm just trying to figure out what took you so long today to walk to the mall and see a movie. You were gone for almost five hours. I know it doesn't take that long to go to the mall and see a movie. I cooked these pizzas nearly two hours ago. I figured you should've been home by then. I don't think you just went to the mall and the movies. You probably went gallivanting all over town."

"We didn't Mom. We just went to the mall and the movies. The movie started late cause we wanted to see the matinee. It's cheaper. That's all we did. Honest."

Sarah defended Karla, "Yeah, Mrs. Centon, we must've spent about an hour in the pet shop looking at all the fish. They've lots of fish. My dad is thinking about setting up an aquarium in our living room. They got lots of really nice fish there."

Jody apologized, "We're sorry, we didn't know the movie was going to be so long."

"Mrs. Centon, we just thought the movie was going to be over before it got dark." Sarah looked at Karla. "So I guess now isn't the time for Karla to ask if she can have a kitten."

Mrs. Centon addressed Karla, "No kittens. No, Cats. No, Dogs. Next time you're going to do something like that and be late; call home before doing it." With that, she got up from the table taking her drink with her into the living room, leaving the girls in peace.

Sarah whispered, "God, Karla. We didn't know she'd be like that."

Karla bit her lip to keep it from trembling. She hated it when her mother spoke to her like that in front of her friends. Her appetite now lost, she wondered if she could get away with throwing out the pizza without her mother noticing.

"Your mom's drinking again, isn't she," Jody nibbled on her pizza.

"Yeah...I guess so... I don't want to talk about it... Not now."

Karla ripped a piece of the pizza off her slice. She slowly chewed it. It was rubbery and cold.

They finished their meal in silence. Karla couldn't wait for this night to be over. She'd that feeling all along that her mom's niceness wouldn't last long.

Sarah noted the time on the clock. It hung on the wall above the kitchen sink. They could see it from where they sat at the table. "We better get our stuff together. My folks will be here soon."

Taking care of their plates, they went to Karla's room quietly. Hoping Mrs. Centon wouldn't notice them gone. In Karla's room, they quickly gathered their things together. They were sorry for getting Karla in trouble with her mom.

Headlights pulled into the driveway. Karla could see them from her bedroom window. Putting her face close to the window, she was able to see the car.

"They're here," Karla announced.

They hugged Karla while the car horn beeped.

"I'm gonna miss you guys…" Karla said sadly.

They took their things to the front door, quickly saying goodbye and thank you to Mrs. Centon for letting them sleep over. Karla accompanied them out the door to see them get into the car. She waved goodbye, saying "Call me."

"Don't forget watch out for that creep," Jody yelled out the car window.

"Yeah, you watch out for Dave, then," Karla shouted back.

"See yah," Jody yelled.

"See yah," Karla shouted back as the car pulled out of the driveway.

"I'll call you," Sarah yelled out the back window. The car pulled out into the street and quickly disappeared from sight.

As soon as the car was out of sight Karla returned inside. She glared at her mom on her way to her room and shut the door just shy of slamming it shut.

She hated her mother. There was no reason she needed to act like she did in front of her friends. It was just not fair. It wasn't like she'd been that late getting home. At least she'd made it back home before eight o'clock.

Karla grabbed her pillow off her bed and hugged it tight against her stomach and bit her lip to hold back the tears and sobs.

Not fair – she wasn't ever fair to her when her friends were involved.

Maybe, just maybe, Karla thought – she picked up her cell phone and tried calling Jan.

It had rung six times before the answering machine picked up. Announcing, "I can't come to the phone right now, please leave your name and number, and I'll get back to you as soon as I can…"

Never mind, thought Karla… She probably would say no anyway…

## 17

THE NEXT DAY KARLA HAD A STUDY HALL DURING HER FIRST PERI-
od. She was able to get a pass from the teacher allowing her to take her study hall in
the library instead of the classroom.

Carol said she'd be going to the library too for her study period and that she'd
meet her there. "If you get there before me, save me a cubicle, and if I get there
before you, I'll save one for you." Carol had said to her when she saw her at her locker
before going to their homeroom for daily attendance.

At her old school, the library was small. They didn't have the privacy cubicles as
they'd at Brantwood High. If they had, Karla was sure she would've done the same
with Jody and Sarah.

"Karla, did you finish the report yet," asked Carol as she dropped her books
down on the cubicle table. Pulling the chair back, she hung her purse on the back and
sat in the chair facing Karla.

The library was lined with wooden cubicles separating students, allowing some
privacy. The school was so large; it allowed the library to be on two levels. Both levels
shelved a vast selection of books and study material. Karla was sure her hometown's
town library wasn't as large as this library.

Big tables were placed in the middle of the library, allowing groups of students
to study together. These were found on both levels along with the numerous cubicles.
Karla and Carol were on the lower level.

"No…but I did start it," Karla said as she looked up from her math homework.
The paper was littered with erase marks. The geometry equations were giving her
some trouble.

"I haven't even thought about mine yet," replied Carol.

She leaned toward Karla to get a better look at what she was working on. Then, leaning back in her chair, she pulled out a notebook with names and sayings strewn across the cover.

"What're you gonna do? It's due Friday," Karla asked while she pushed away the math paper and tossed her pencil down on the table before her. She was frustrated and knew she'd never get her math homework done. It had to be turned in next block.

"I don't know, maybe I'll turn it in next week," Carol said while she pulled a note out of her notebook. Smiling, she pushed the note off to the side and ripped a page out of her notebook.

"Doesn't she mark it down for each day it is late," Karla asked.

"Yeah, but that's okay…It'll pass."

Carol began to write a note.

"My folks get mad if I don't get anything but A's and B's." Karla picked the pencil back up and pulled the math paper back in front of her. She had to get this done before the period was over. Holding the paper up, she began to concentrate on that geometry equation giving her trouble.

"Mine gave up on me a long time ago. Now they're just happy if I pass."

Carol began to fold her finished note into a football. She wrote Heath's name on the outside of it.

"So what're you going to do after you graduate?

My folks said I can't get into college unless I've good grades," Karla said as she set the math paper back down and began to scribble part of the equation down.

"College…Bah… If I go to college, it'll be on a volleyball scholarship. Academics aren't my strongest thing…I like doing the sports thing."

Carol turned around in the chair to check the clock on the wall. They still had another half an hour before the next period.

"And your folks are okay with that," Karla asked. She was miffed. She wished her folks were like that. Then there wouldn't be any pressure or stress to make the grade.

"What choice do they've anyway?

It's my life. Maybe I'll just get married and have kids," Carol grinned.

"I don't know…I want to do something with my life."

But it'd be nice if she could make her own decisions about what she wanted to do with her life. Her mom was always saying she had to take this course or take that class because she had to go to Condorf College, which was only an hour away from Brantwood.

Karla tried to focus on the math paper again. She scratched down letters and symbols on the paper before her.

"What're you gonna do after you graduate," Carol asked as she sucked on the end of her pencil.

"Go to college and do something in the medical field."

At least, that was what Karla's mom wanted her to do. On the other hand, Karla would rather be an elementary teacher.

"Oh. Good luck, then."

Carol pulled out her science book. Another note fell out of the pages. There was also a test folded in the pages showing a C- grade on it.

Karla worked on the next ten questions without any interruption. She erased the last equation several times before finding the answer. Looking at the clock she saw that she'd ten minutes till next block. She was so glad she was able to finish the math homework in time.

Maggie passed behind them and tossed a note on Carol's table. Carol unfolded it to read it.

"Hey, do you party," Carol asked.

"Party," repeated Karla. She was bewildered by the question.

"Yeah, you know, hang out with friends…have a couple of drinks… Maybe dance, talk and chill."

"I've never been to one – no one ever asked me to one before," Karla said while she stuffed her books into her backpack.

"Wanna go? There is gonna be one at Ian's this Friday. His dad has to go out-of-town, and he'll have the house to himself." Carol began to gather up her things as well.

"I don't know." Karla turned in the chair to face Carol.

"Come on, it'll be fun."

"My folks probably won't let me go."

Both mall incidents were still in the back of her mind. Carol shoplifting, and her mom yelling at her for coming home late with Sarah and Jody on Sunday.

"Don't tell them. Say that you're sleeping over at my house."

"I don't know…I'll have to get back to you." Karla hated being pressured.

"Why? You already got plans," Carol snipped.

"Um…I just got to get back to you."

"I think Gerry is going."

"Oh?" The mention of Gerry being there caught Karla's interest.

"I hear he's free again," Carol whispered.

Karla tipped her head. "So what're you saying?" She couldn't understand why Carol was so intent on this party thing.

"You like him, right," Carol smiled, "Like no one hasn't noticed."

"Yeah…" Karla knew her cheeks glowed red hot.

"So ask him out, silly," Carol snickered.

"Oh…I don't know," Karla said softly. "I don't think he'd go out with me."

"You won't know unless you ask," Carol grinned knowingly.

"I don't know…I don't think I can ask him."

"You can, it's easy. Just walk up to him and ask."

"That's easy for you to say you're pretty outgoing." Karla stood up and slipped her backpack over her shoulder. The school bell rang for the next period.

"All right – think about it, but don't wait too long, or he'll be taken again. I'll even help you ask him. Why don't you see if you can make plans to come over to my house after school tomorrow, and we can go over a plan to get you to the party with Gerry?"

"I'll think about it," Karla reluctantly agreed, "I got to go to class…I'll talk to you later."

The rest of the school day went by without a hitch. There was no test in her math class, so that made the day much better. She was able to take lunch again with Carol, but she couldn't help notice the whispering taking place at the table.

Left out, as though she were the target of some sort of joke or something, it made her wonder if there was a problem in this school with hazing. She decided to keep her suspicions to herself for now. Hazing or no hazing, she wasn't going to fall apart before these new friends of hers. This seemed to be the crowd to be with.

Karla went straight home after school. She did her best to avoid her mother. Her dad had left her the chore of mowing the grass.

She found the mower in the shed beside the pool house, and she mowed the small portion of the grass in the back yard.

She thought to herself of how she could've used a pair of scissors on the patch because it was so small. But then again, that'd've been too much trouble... The mower was after all the easiest way to go.

Her dad was not home for supper that night. Karla ate in silence. She avoided looking at her mother or engaging in any conversation with her.

As soon as they were done eating, Karla excused herself from the table. She used the excuse of having lots of homework to do. She didn't even dare ask if she could go to Carol's after school tomorrow, she feared another confrontation since her mom sat once again with one of those drinks before her.

Karla so hated it when her mom drank that stuff. She became so irritable and moody, and Karla could never say or do anything right.

Mrs. Centon fumed to herself after Karla ran off to her bedroom.

"That child never helps me with the dishes, never helps clean the house and she refuses to acknowledge my existence. And, she wonders why I drink... Moments like these... and she wonders why."

# 18

THE NEXT MORNING, KARLA, WOKE WITH A START. THE ALARM
clock was blaring Snoop Dog. She reached over to slam the button off, knocking it off
the nightstand.

All night, she could not think of anything else but the party and Gerry. This kept
her from falling asleep. She tossed and turned, thinking of how her parents would
deny her the freedom to go to such an event. She could hear her Mom saying, "Are
there going to be any parents there? Whom are you going to be with? I don't think
so. I'm sure there is drinking at the party, and drugs too. You're not going, and that's
final."

Karla feared what she was going to tell Carol. She would probably think she was
some sort of dweeb, and not let her hang with them anymore.

She grabbed a shirt from her dresser drawer and quickly pulled it on over her
head. Looking in her mirror on her bedroom door, she checked the fit of the shirt.
The neckline was low, but it would pass the school dress code. The jeans, Karla, picked
out were of a tight fit hip-hugger. Not quite as tight as wearing skinny jeans.

She checked her behind in the mirror to make sure her underwear was not showing before leaving her bedroom. She knew her mom would send her right back into
her room to change if even just a little bit of waistband was showing.

When she hurried to the bathroom, she checked to see the whereabouts of her
mom. She thought it was strange that her mom had not called out to her to see if she
was up yet. Puzzled by her mom's absence, she hurried back into her room collecting
her backpack before leaving for school.

She checked her time on her clock and saw that she needed to hurry, or she
would be late for school. With her backpack swung over her shoulder, she made sure
she shut her bedroom door behind her. Her bed was still unmade.

Stopping in the kitchen, she saw there was still no sign of her mom. Karla
thought this was very odd, maybe she was still sleeping. Karla took the opportunity
to grab a box of orange juice from the fridge to drink on her way to school. A lonely

muffin sat wrapped on the counter with a note tucked under it. She picked up the note and read:

Karla,

I had to go watch Amy this morning. Her mom is in the hospital having her baby. I left you a muffin on the counter in case you would like one. See you when you get home from school.

Love,

Mom

"Cool, Mom's not here," Karla said out loud. She snatched up the muffin and tossed its wrapper into the trash. She left for school, locking the door behind her. What an uneventful morning. Maybe things would work out after all. She couldn't believe how the morning was turning out. It was such a nice day today too. Not even a cloud in the sky. If the weather continued to be nice, she could get used to the daily walk to school.

Karla noticed the crowds of students gathered at the entrance of the school. They would sit on the school steps or stand next to cars in the parking lot. The biggest group was Carol's group of friends. Karla quickly gave the group a glance to see if Carol was amongst them. She was not. Maybe she was already inside.

On the way to her locker, Karla still did not see Carol. She began to wonder if she was coming to school today. Maybe she was just running late.

Carol skipped up behind Karla while she placed her stuff in her locker. "So. Are you gonna go to the party, or what?"

Her sudden appearance startled Karla and the sound of her voice made her jump. "I don't know yet – I haven't asked my folks." She took the books she need for the next two classes and slammed the locker shut.

"Why do you need to ask them? Just tell them you're sleeping over my house." Carol leaned with her back up against the lockers. "I'm really sure Gerry will go to the party with you."

"I'm working on it. I will get back with you tomorrow." Karla pulled away from the lockers, leaving for her class, Carol following her down the hallway.

"Hey, can you help me with my history report?"

"I guess so." Karla slipped into the classroom just as the bell rang, setting her books on her desk and taking her seat.

"I thought you wanted me to come over this afternoon."

"Oh yeah – about that, we have to do that tomorrow. I have some stuff I need to take care of. Can you come over tomorrow instead?"

"Yeah, I guess." Karla was off the hook since she never did get around to asking her mom about going to Carol's today, after-school.

Gerry swung around in his chair to address Carol. "Hey – You're going to Ian's

Friday?" He smiled that cute smile that made Karla's heart melt and skip a beat. She was almost sure the smile was really for her. Her face felt hot, so she turned to look out the window, hoping he did not notice her blushing.

Carol snickered. "Of course – I wouldn't miss it for a minute."

Karla could not wait for the day to be over. History class went well. Except for the part where Gerry sat in front of her, and she could not take her eyes off of him. Carol looked over at her a couple of times while she was gazing at him, and let out a small snicker. Karla could feel her face immediately become red.

At lunch, Carol was still being really nice to Karla. But the other girls kept up their whispering. It made Karla feel nervous. She wondered why they were pressuring her so much to go to this party on Friday.

Gerry sat at the other end of the lunch table with the guys. He would look in Karla's direction occasionally and smile at her. Her heart would skip a beat every time she looked up to see him looking in her direction. Maybe there was nothing to this party, and he really did want to go to it with her.

Math and Digital Imaging were the only two classes where Karla didn't seem to struggle with the length of the day. All the other classes just dragged, making it seem that time appeared to stand still.

In Math, there was a test, which took the whole class. While in Digital Imaging, it was just plain fun. Karla really loved that class.

When the last bell rang, signifying the end of the school day, Karla hurried to her locker and tossed most of her books inside on the top shelf. With a quick kick of her foot, the locker door was shut. The day was done, and now she just wanted to be home. But then there was her mom, the thought of her just ruined her mood, making Karla slow her jog down the school steps.

From a distance, Karla could see Gerry standing next to his car in the parking lot. He was surrounded by a large group of his and Carol's friends. Carol was nowhere in sight. Karla wondered why Carol couldn't meet her after school today.

Karla avoided the group. As she passed by, Maggie gave a look that made Karla feel uncomfortable, more like a glare. Gerry didn't seem to notice the look. He let his gaze follow Karla while she walked by, smiling at her. Karla gave a slight smile back and hurried on her way.

Now she seemed to walk faster on her way home from school even though she wasn't really in much of a hurry. Gerry's smile had energized her. Maybe he really did want to go to the party with her after all.

Karla was surprised when her driveway suddenly appeared in front of her. She didn't even remember crossing the street. But that didn't really matter. What mattered was that the driveway was empty. This meant her mom was not home yet, and she was glad. After producing a key from a pocket of her backpack, Karla let herself into the house, taking refuge in her room.

Later on that night, Karla was happy of how uneventful dinner turned out. Her dad made it home for supper, but they all ate pretty much in silence. Her mom spoke about Amy's mom. She did not have her baby yet, and the doctors were going to induce her labor tomorrow.

After tending to the dishes with her dad, Karla took refuge again in her room. She almost asked about going to Carol's on Friday, but she was just not ready to ask. Maybe she would ask tomorrow. Hopefully her dad would be home again, and she would be able to ask and convince him. He was her best bet at letting her go out that night.

# 19

THOUGHTS OF THE PARTY NAGGED KARLA ALL NIGHT. SHE TOSSED
and turned in her sleep. Her dreams were of her parents walking into the house where
the party was being held, and screaming at her and all her friends. It was a nightmare
of her mom chasing all the kids out the door, and her dad threatening them with
calling the police.

In her dream her mom was yelling at her, "So where are his parents? You told us
a parent would be here. You're grounded, young lady."

The last thing she remembered about the dream was her dad yelling, "Go home
now, before I carry you home."

Karla sat up in her bed, it was still dark out. She looked over at her alarm clock.
She could see that there were another three hours to go until it was time to get up. She
lay back down and tried to get back to sleep, but the sleep would just not come.

So she gave up and snapped on her table lamp beside her bed, and began to
ponder how she was going to get permission to go to Carol's on Friday night. She was
starting to fear that this party thing was not such a good idea. It was almost like a gut
feeling or something.

Knowing her mother was again leaving early to babysit Amy, Karla waited until
she heard her Mom call out to her, saying she was leaving. Having already dressed, she
slipped out of her room as soon as she saw her mom's car pull out of the driveway
and drive up the street.

A piece of toast would be good enough for breakfast.

While she was buttering her toast, she schemed about how she could meet with
Carol after school today. The more she thought about it, the better it sounded to her.
She'd leave her mom a note. It was to let her know that she needed to meet Carol after
school today, so she could help her with her History report.

And while she was with Carol, she could help her come up with a plan to get her
folks to let her stay at Carol's on Friday night.

Karla smiled. Her plan seemed to be perfect and not too far-fetched. She quickly found the pad of paper and jotted down her after-school plans.

Mom,

      I forgot to tell you. I have to stop at the library on my way home from school today. Carol asked me if I'd help her with the History report. And I need a bit more research to finish up my report. I promise to be home by 5.

Karla

Satisfied with her note, Karla left it pinned to the fridge with a magnet. The fridge was bare of any other notes. Pictures no longer cluttered the door surface. Karla had ended this ritual of hanging her school papers on the refrigerator years ago.

She wondered when the last time she'd hung a picture on it. It must've been back when she was in fourth or fifth grade. That seemed so long ago.

She made sure the note was at eye level on the door. She just hoped her mom would see it before school got out.

Karla left for school, a bit more upbeat. Maybe Amy's mom had her baby today. She hoped it was a boy. Amy really wanted a little brother.

The day seemed to be certainly looking up for her. Maybe her mom wouldn't even be home when she got out of school. Maybe she'd have to stay the night at Amy's. But Karla knew she couldn't be that lucky.

At school, Karla wove her way around the students standing outside the entrance. Seeing Gerry enter the building before her, she slowed up and followed him at a distance.

He stopped at Carol's locker, slipping a note into the vent at the top. He gave a quick glance around, looking like he was checking to see if Carol was coming. Then he spotted Heath across the hall.

Karla quickly looked away, hoping he didn't notice her watching him. Just the sight of him made her heart race. She opened her locker to put her things away. Once again Carol slipped in behind her and snagged a notebook out of her locker.

"What the hell," Karla snapped, Carol's sudden action stunning her.

"I just wanted to help," Carol said. She held out the notebook for Karla to take back.

"You made me jump, I hate it when people come up behind me like that," Karla accepted the notebook.

"Hey – did you or didn't you make up your mind yet about the party? Ian needs to know so he can plan on who's coming."

"Yeah…I want to go. But you need to help me with what I'm gonna tell my folks." She gathered her books into her arms. "So how 'bout after school today, we meet at the library downtown, and we can go over it, and I'll help you with your report?" Karla shut her locker.

"Sounds good to me, I don't have practice today, so it'll work."

Carol leaned her back against the lockers, giving thumbs up to the group of guys standing in the hallway.

Karla saw Ian wave back. Gerry grinned, looking in her direction. Apparently, a joke was being passed among the crowd. Karla looked away. She couldn't help notice the group of girls walking up the hallway, Carol's friends.

"Darcy, you going to the party," Carol shouted out to one of the girls in the group. She looked back at Karla and said, "I'll see you later in class."

Karla watched Carol move off with the group of girls. Giggling, they made their way back down the hallway whence they came.

Shaking her head, Karla headed on her way to her first class. She was disturbed by the way Carol blew her off for her other friends. But what was she supposed to expect, she was the newcomer wasn't she?

The morning seemed to go by fast. Before Karla knew it, it was lunchtime. Looking at her schedule, she saw her lunch was later today. She'd a feeling she wouldn't be eating lunch with Carol and her friends.

Stopping at her locker to get her lunch, Karla saw Carol in the hallway, "…you going to lunch now?"

"No…I already had lunch. I was looking for you," Carol answered. "You still want to meet at the library after school?"

"Yeah, of course," Karla snapped the locker shut.

"We might have to meet tomorrow…I might have practice after all…I'll get back to you during last period. I should know by then," Carol said as she began walking away, heading in the direction of her next class down the hallway.

"Sure," Karla called after her.

The cafeteria was packed, as usual. Karla looked around the room to see if she saw any familiar faces from any of her classes. Spotting two girls from her Digital Imaging class, she made her way over to them.

They were sitting by themselves. One girl had long black hair that was tied back against her head in a bun. A pencil was sticking through the center of it, holding it in place. She was dressed as a Goth.

The other girl, who sat across from her, wore red framed glasses which matched her short wavy red hair. When she smiled, her braces showed their silver tracks across her teeth. She looked like she could be someone's secretary, except for the black finger nail polish. A Goth wanna be Karla guessed.

"Can I join you," Karla asked the gothic dressed girls.

"Do you really want to sit with us?" The other girl replied. She put a finger on her glasses and pushed them higher up her nose with her black fingernails, which looked odd on her fingers.

"Sure, why not," Karla set her lunch down on the table and took a seat next to the girl with the black hair.

"We just thought you were one of Carol's friends," the red haired girl replied.

"Yeah, she's one of my friends."

Karla opened her lunch bag, taking out a bologna and cheese sandwich. This was the third time this week she had to have a bologna and cheese sandwich. Didn't her mom know she didn't like bologna and cheese sandwiches?

She took the sandwich out of its bag and bit into it anyway.

"Don't let her see you hanging with us or she won't be your friend for long if she does."

"She doesn't like us...I don't know why...She just never has."

"Well, I guess I'll sit with you, then," Karla said, "and she'll have to live with it." She took another bite of her sandwich.

"Okay, we warned you. By the way, I didn't catch your name in class the other day. I'm Jerra," the gothic dressed girl pulled a notebook from her bag and opened it. The heading on the page was News.

"I'm Karla. Do you work on the school newspaper," she asked as she nodded toward the open notebook.

"We both do. I'm Marla...You wouldn't be interested in joining the student newspaper group, would you? We need more photographers."

"Hmm, it actually does sound interesting. When do you meet," Karla asked.

"Well, since most of the games take place Fridays after school," Jerra said. "We like to meet on Saturdays and gather the info, so we can have the paper ready to publish first thing Monday morning."

"I think I'd really like to join. Where do you meet?"

Karla stuffed her empty sandwich bag into her disposable water bottle.

"Great," Marla said, "Meet us in the lower room at the town library 9:00 Saturday morning. And bring your camera. Try to make the game on Friday night, and take some pictures of the game and the crowd," Jerra said as she got up to take her lunch tray away to dispose of her trash.

"Sounds great, then I'll see you Saturday morning, then."

The lunch bell rang. Karla gathered up her books and headed off to class. She dropped her trash into the bucket on her way out the cafeteria door.

Karla couldn't help but think about being in on the student newspaper group. She couldn't wait to tell Sarah and Jody. Maybe Jody would teach her about football, or perhaps she could ask her dad. He'd definitely know what she needed to learn, she was sure of it. He watched all the games when he was home, well at least the pro football games. She wasn't too sure about him watching any of the college games.

Her last class of the day finally arrived. It had been a long week. Or maybe it was because she just couldn't wait until Friday night, so much was going on now. First, she'd to go to the game, then a party, and on Saturday, the newspaper meeting. How much better could it get?

She sat daydreaming through Biology class, imagining what the weekend would be like, trying to scheme and make plans. There was the nagging in the back of her mind, reminding her that she still had to work on the plan of getting permission from her parents for Friday night. But she was sure Carol would have an answer to the problem.

Karla still hadn't seen Carol since just before lunch. She didn't know if they were still on for meeting at the library after school. Not knowing if she should head to the library and wait for Carol, she decided to stop at her locker to exchange the books she didn't need for homework. Opening her locker, Karla saw the note fall out of the locker and onto the floor.

Picking up the note, she opened it up to read:

Karla,

Hey... I got practice this afternoon ... so let's meet tomorrow at the library instead. K ... see yah tomorrow in class.

Carol

Karla stuffed the note into her pocket and, slipped the backpack over her shoulder. Disappointed by the note, she walked home.

The sights and sounds of the bustling busy street captured Karla's attention. She paused at the stoplight to watch that little old lady she saw on the street the day her family moved to town. She was still pushing that shopping cart around. Seeing her again made Karla wonder what it was like to be homeless.

The walk light changed to "walk". Karla forgot all about the old lady. She followed the crowd across the street.

Karla couldn't believe how quickly she walked home. She turned the corner onto her street after passing the corner store. The store didn't seem too busy right now.

After she passed the third house on her street, she could see her mom's car in the driveway. She'd been hoping her mom wasn't going to be home yet.

Her mom greeted her as she walked in the door.

"Karla, I thought you were going to go to the library after school today," her mom questioned, "did you at least remember to pick up your research material?"

"Oh, hi Mom," Karla shifted her backpack from her shoulder to her forearm, "Did Amy's mom have her baby?"

"Yes, she'd a little boy. He was born at 8:29 this morning."

"Oh cool." Karla searched her mom's face trying to sense what kind of mood she was in. "That's what Amy was hoping for."

"I'll be going back there again tomorrow to watch Amy again. Her mom won't be home for another day."

"Okay. Tell her I said congrats. Oh, and I didn't go to the library today, 'cause Carol had volleyball practice. We're going to meet there tomorrow after-school instead."

Mrs. Centon nodded. She suddenly remembered something she'd meant to bring to Karla's attention the other day, "Oh when you mowed the lawn the other day, you were supposed to mow the front yard too. Please get it done tonight."

"Okay," Karla said sourly. There was always something her mom would find to complain about, Karla knew this was coming.

She pushed her way past her mom and into her bedroom. Her homework would have to wait for now. She checked her phone to see if there were any messages. There were none. She'd texted Sarah about the newspaper club earlier, but she'd still gotten no response.

"Time to mow the lawn again," she grumbled to herself.

# 20

THE NEXT DAY, KARLA WALKED EXCITEDLY TO HER LOCKER. SHE saw Carol in the hallway and made a beeline straight for her. She noticed the girls gathered around Carol all scattered at her approach.

"Carol, hey, I talked to my Mom. I can sleep over at your house on Friday," Karla said excitedly. She'd made sure she mowed the lawn as best as she could and she did a little bit of housework for her mom too. She did all this before trying to convince her into letting her sleepover Carol's on Friday.

They'd even argued over it a little bit. But, her mom finally gave in; this was only after Karla pointed out to her that she was almost 17. She'd be 17 in like, ten more months. Then her mom went into a panic, thinking Karla was looking to take drivers ed. next. Karla had reassured her that she'd no interest in learning to drive yet.

"Oh – right – high. Hey, can you still help me with my report today after school," Carol said with a smile.

Karla couldn't help but notice how weird Carol's eyes looked. They looked bloodshot and squinted like she didn't get enough sleep or something. Or maybe it was something else. She began to wonder. Nah, she thought. She's on the Volleyball team, and she's the Team Captain. She wouldn't do something like that. Or would she?

Karla moved over to her locker to take some books from it. "Yeah…Of course I can." She couldn't help but notice the strange look in Carol's eyes.

"You feel okay? Your eyes look really weird."

"Oh… I think I'm coming down with a cold or something. I'll be all right. So, we can meet at the library after school, right," Carol asked as she opened up her locker and checked her eyes out in her mirror on the door. She pocketed a small bottle and slammed it shut.

Trying not to be evident, Karla tried to get a glimpse of the bottle before she slipped it into her pocket. Failing to see what it was, she grabbed her books for class. "Yeah…I'll meet ya after school. You can think of a way for me to ask Gerry out."

"You should just ask Gerry to go to the party with you, plain and simple," Carol said while she lingered, waiting for Karla.

"I don't know…I have to work up my nerve to do something like that…, it's my first party, and all," Karla replied. She looked around, wary of anyone listening in on the conversation, relieved to see the hallway was empty.

"We'll talk about it more, later...I got to go to class..., see-yah later," Carol called to her as she made her way down the hallway.

Karla dragged through another long day at school. She ended up eating lunch again with Jerra and Marla. She thought how much alike they seem to be to her old friends, Sarah, and Jody. The thought of them made her miss them.

Sarah had sent Karla a text message just before lunch, giving her the thumbs up about the newspaper club. She said she thought how cool the idea was of Karla taking photos for the school newspaper.

Karla never once mentioned the party to Sarah. She was afraid she'd try to talk her out of going to it.

Again Jerra and Marla warned Karla about Carol. But Karla reassured them, saying she could handle Carol and her friends.

She was not about to back down now from that group. She feared if she didn't go to that party, things could become very miserable for her at this school. If this was going to be hazing, she was not going to back down. She couldn't.

After-school, Carol didn't cancel their meeting at the library as the two previous days. Karla did wonder if she'd show up at the library. After all, Carol really didn't seem to care about school work.

The library was only a few blocks from Karla's house. She hurried home to drop off the books she didn't need, bringing only her history book and the notebook she kept her report in. She rushed past her mom sitting in the living room.

"Karla, where are you going," her mom asked quickly.

"Got to go, Mom," Karla showed her mom the history book. "I've to do a bit more on my report, so I'm going to the library. And remember, I've to help Carol with her history report. I'll be back soon."

"Don't be late for supper."

Karla quickly shut the front door behind her, nervously. Slipping out of the house without asking for permission to go somewhere was just not like her. But, in a way she'd already asked for permission yesterday, so she really shouldn't feel guilty about running out the door the way she was.

She nervously glanced over her shoulder back at her house. The adrenaline coursing through her body, Karla just couldn't believe she'd done that and gotten away with it. Turning the corner onto Main Street, she hurried on her way to the library.

But the more she thought about it, she really didn't get away with anything. She did ask for permission yesterday afternoon. She relaxed some. Maybe she was just nervous about going to the party tomorrow. Yeah, that's it. Fooling her parents into believing she was just sleeping over Carol's, had to be what was troubling her.

The library loomed before her on the left. Karla could see Carol sitting on the library steps. She looked like she was lounging. Karla snickered, thinking Carol looked funny.

A group of pedestrians was waiting for the streetlight to change so they could cross the street. Karla quickly joined them at the back of the group. When the light turned, she followed the surge forward. Cars lined up on both sides of the street, waiting for the light. She heard vibrating bass-beating rap from one of the cars.

Moving quickly past the group of pedestrians, Karla reached the library steps faster than she anticipated. Almost out of breath from walking so rapidly, she hurried up the steps.

"That was fast," Carol greeted.

"Are you ready to get started," Karla asked as she slowed down her breathing, trying to mask her loss of breath.

Carol stood up and followed Karla into the library.

"You didn't bring any books, paper, or pencils?"

Carol shook her head.

"Glad I brought mine."

Karla led the way to a large table and placed her things on it. Carol pulled out a chair and sat down. Taking the seat next to Carol, Karla sat down and opened up her notebook.

"What's your report on?"

"Um, the Civil War, I think," Carol answered. "I don't know…I don't remember."

"'Since you didn't start it yet, I take it…. It'll be the Civil War, then."

Karla jotted the heading across the top of the paper.

"Now we've to go look up information on the Civil War."

Karla took Carol around the library to show her where to find the catalog. She found that Carol had no idea what it was or how to use one. After a long process of explaining the catalog, she brought Carol around the library, showing her where the books were located.

Collecting the books, Karla piled them up in Carol's arms; six books would give her more than enough information. After she had ushered Carol back to the table, she said, "Here, let me see." She took a book from Carol's pile.

Carol picked up the pencil and waited. She cupped her head in her hand with her elbow on the table. "I don't know what to write."

"Here, put this down, but in your own words." She pushed a book in front of Carol, exposing the article on the page.

"Can't I just copy it?"

"No. She'll know you didn't write it. You can use these to write your report. Just change the words to your own."

"So, you want me to write all that," Carol asked as she slumped back in her chair, looking like she was ready to give up.

"No, just use some of it. The report only has to be five hundred words," Karla said encouragingly.

She watched as Carol jotted down a few sentences. Carol would pause; start to write again, then only to erase what she'd written.

Carol suddenly looked up from her paper.

"Oh…Hey, I know how you can ask Gerry to the party."

"Huh? Oh, yeah. Are you sure he's gonna want to go to it with me?"

Karla looked up from a book she was flipping through.

"Yes. Silly. He has study period in the library, and he still hasn't finished his report. He'll be there by himself. Ask him then. If you want, I can talk to him first. I can give you some sort of signal letting you know the coast is clear."

"I don't know..."

"Think about it, and get back with me. Don't wait too long, or someone else will ask him out," Carol said while she drummed the pencil eraser against her chin.

"I'll think about it...Hey, I got to get going—it's starting to get dark. I'll see ya in school tomorrow." Last thing she wanted was a repeat of Sunday night. Karla picked up her notebook. She pulled a few more sheets of paper from it and set them on the table before Carol.

"You can have the pencil. I've plenty more."

"Thanks for your help."

Carol once again slumped back in her chair.

Karla hurriedly said, "Yup, I'll see you tomorrow," as she pushed her chair back from the table, leaving Carol to work on the report by herself. Stepping out of the library, she noted the sun was beginning to set. She looked at the time on her cell phone and saw that it was getting late. She had to hurry. Supper would be ready in about fifteen minutes.

# 21

KARLA LEFT THE HOUSE AS FAST AS SHE COULD. SHE SLIPPED PAST her mom standing in the kitchen. Carefully, she closed the front door as quietly as she could.

Power-walking as fast as she could, Karla was determined to tell Carol of her decision. She was ready to ask Gerry out, but she was jittery. She was anxious and worried about him possibly saying no.

She'd taken extra special care of choosing her wardrobe this morning, picking out a nice low cut top that enhanced her brown eyes. She was not used to wearing skirts, but today would be an appropriate day to wear one. It'd been suggested by Carol yesterday while she was helping her with her history report.

She'd found a nice skirt in her closet. It was a short denim one. One she'd forgotten about owning. It must've been sitting on that hanger since last May.

She was glad her mom never noticed her slipping out the door wearing it. She'd have known Karla was up to something. Since Karla rarely ever wore any dresses or skirts.

Carol was at her locker. Darcy and Maggie were leaning on each side of it, talking to her. Darcy smiled at Karla's approach, but Maggie glared at her.

"Hi, Karla," they chimed together and walked away to another group of students gathered in the hall, giving Carol her privacy she'd wanted for this moment.

Karla was glad they didn't stay to hear her tell Carol of her plans.

"You're early," Carol noted.

"Yeah…I guess. Did you finish your report?" Karla asked.

"Almost," replied Carol with a grin. She pulled the paper from her history book to show what she'd done. The page was half written on.

"Well, that's a start, anyway," Karla said as she handed back the paper.

Oh, God, can I do this? Karla asked herself as she opened her locker and shoved her books into it. She looked around to see if anyone was in hearing range. Satisfied, she spoke up.

"Hey, Carol…I think I can do it. You said you'd talk to him first."

"Um, yeah… Sure. I have to go to the library before next block. You got time?"

"Yeah, I got a study period. I requested a pass to the library today," Karla replied.

"Um… Then this is what we'll do. When I put my hand up to my hair and pull it back like this," She demonstrated. "You come walking down the library stairs and take the seat next to him, and then just make small talk with him first."

Karla looked around nervously. She was unnatural in the skirt. Already she was missing her jeans. And she hoped she wouldn't trip wearing these heels. Even though they were low heels, they were heels just the same. Sneakers were her foot ware of choice besides flip-flops.

Carol smiled and continued. "But when you come to the library I want you to wait up on the upper level. Where you can see me at the booths. Wait for my signal."

"See you in a bit, then," Karla said as she nervously fled up the hallway. Her panic almost caused her to bump into Heath. Giggling nervously, she slipped into the classroom to take her seat for roll call.

She listened to the buzz chattering around the room. The big event of the week was Ian's party. Karla caught a glimpse of Jerra passing by in the hallway. "I've to re-member — Saturday newspaper meeting. This is gonna be a great weekend," She said quietly to herself.

Homeroom bell rang. The students quieted down, waiting for the morning an-nouncements. A reminder of the football game after school was made. Karla couldn't wait for homeroom to be over. She kept smoothing her skirt down, inspecting it for any lint.

The sound of the bell ringing didn't bring her any relief. Karla was more nervous than before. She waited for the other students to leave the class before her. She then made her way to the library, finding the spot on the upper level of the library where Carol had told her to stand. She waited for the signal. She watched Carol take her place at the booth below.

She waited for almost 10 minutes. Pretending to look for study material while keeping an eye on where Carol and Gerry sat. She was over conscious about the outfit she was wearing. She hoped it wasn't too outdated. Fashion changes so fast. It was hard to keep one's wardrobe up to date.

Then it happened. She saw the movement at the cubicles below.

Catching the signal from Carol, Karla brushed her skirt, took a deep breath, and walked towards where Gerry sat. She carefully maneuvered the stairs; scared she might trip and make a scene.

Other students filled the library during their free study period, gathering at tables, sitting in booths, or looking for research materials for various reports. She walked past a table, to where he sat in a booth.

"Is anyone sitting here," Karla asked him. She admired the way the wisps of curls hung over his brow.

"No. Carol had to go back to class," Gerry replied. He quickly glanced at her, only to return his focus back to his report.

Karla set her things down in the next booth.

"You haven't finished that yet? It's due today."

Karla tried to push her shyness aside to make small talk, as Carol suggested.

"What do you want? You're bugging me."

He flipped the paper over so she couldn't see what he'd written. Pencil between his thumb and forefinger, he began to tap the eraser on the surface in front of him.

"There's a party at Ian's tonight—do yah want to go to it with me," Karla blurt out nervously. She feared he could see how nervous she was. I can't believe I'm doing this, she thought.

Gerry leaned back in his chair. The pencil continued tapping. His eyes locked on hers. A smile formed across his face. Karla's heart skipped a beat. She knew her face must be flushed.

Gerry reached out and touched the top of her hand. The movement startled Karla. She never expected his touch.

"I guess I can go," he finally said. "My parents will be going away for the weekend. You want me to pick you up," he asked as she smiled sheepishly.

A movement caught Gerry's attention. Karla allowed her eyes to look in the direction Gerry was looking. His friends, Justin, and Heath entered the library. They were headed in their direction. Karla noted the time on the clock above the check-out desk.

Smiling, Karla quickly picked up her things at the sound of the bell ringing for the next class.

"Sure. I'll be ready and waiting."

She hurried away and almost bumped into Justin. She clumsily scooted past Heath and out the door, into the hallway.

Karla knew eyes on her when she walked away. She purposely wore the skirt, at Carol's suggestion—a skirt having a nice short length. Carol said it'd be a sight he and his buddies would enjoy seeing. Karla believed it would be an outfit Gerry wouldn't be able to resist.

Sure enough, it was, even his buddies couldn't resist—she knew for sure when she caught their heads turning when she passed them in the hall.

Maybe I should dress like this more often. I wonder how they'd behave if I bent over, she chuckled to herself.

# 22

KARLA MADE HER WAY INTO HISTORY CLASS, AND SHE NOTED CAR-
ol sitting at her desk on the other side of the classroom. She took her place at her
desk and turned toward Carol. She gave her the thumbs-up sign. She then turned to
face the front of the room again, pushing her book toward the left corner of her desk
as she slouched back in her chair.

Excited about the evening, Karla began to worry about her parents changing
their minds about letting her spend the night at Carol's for the sleepover. God, I hope
my parents don't find out about the party. Her stomach was beginning to feel like it
was knotting up inside her.

If they found out, she'd probably be grounded for the rest of her high-school
years. She could see it now.

Anticipation was building up inside her. She wanted to scream her plan to the
world—the thought of spending the evening with Gerry, the captain of the football
team, and she was not even a cheerleader.

Oh God, I can't wait.

She thought about one of the girls back in her old school. Debbie used to tease
Karla about not having a boyfriend. She used to bully Karla too, ever since they started school together in the first grade.

She'd never dreamed of making so many new friends in her first week at this new
school. She was on top of the world at this point. She wished Debbie and her scum
friends could see her now.

Hah. Look at me now. Take that you bitch, she wished she could yell to Debbie
and her friends.

Karla sat through the rest of the class gloating. It never even occurred to her that
Gerry was not in class.

\*\*\*

Carol saw how happy and excited Karla was over the plans for the night. She turned and told in soft whispers the plans to her friends sitting next to her. She'd no intention of telling Karla what she'd in store for her that night.

This was something they did to all the new students who moved into the town from the surrounding area. Their high-school rivals. Why should they be nice to them? Their football, soccer, volleyball and hockey teams were the best in the state. Rivals from the area towns didn't belong in this school, and they needed to go back to where they came from. And anyway, Maggie was just beside herself about Gerry having eyes for Karla. Carol couldn't understand what Maggie was so jealous about. There were five other guys who wanted to go out with her at any given time.

The plans they made were of what they'd be doing before the party. The girls grinned and giggled with Carol over the plans while occasionally glancing at Karla.

# 23

THE DISMISSAL BELL RANG FOR THE END OF THE SCHOOL DAY. THE weekend was finally here. All the students gathered their things and headed out of the classroom, toward lockers or after-school activities.

Karla made her way out the main door, carrying a pile of books. She was surprised she didn't see Carol or Gerry waiting to walk home with her. She shrugged it off and eagerly made her way home, all the while watching the traffic on Main Street, looking for Gerry's car to pass by.

Karla surprised herself. She never realized she could walk so fast.

Her mom's car pulled into the driveway when she passed the third house on her street.

Walking into the house, Karla quickly walked past her mom. She hoped her mom wouldn't change her mind about the sleepover. She didn't linger in the kitchen; she wanted to avoid her mom as much as possible. Just in case.

She headed straight for her room and set her books on her bed. Closing her bedroom door, she picked up her cell phone and called Carol.

"Hey – are we still on for tonight? I didn't see you after school."

Karla was just a bit worried. Maybe the whole party was some sort of prank, especially with all the whispering going on all week long.

"Everything is all set," Carol reassured her. "My folks said it's all right. I told them we'll be going to the movies tonight. So if your parents call mine, they'll tell them that we're at the movies if they ask....

Hey, I got to go. I've to clean my room before you get over here, or my folks will say the whole thing is off for tonight."

"I'll see yah later, then. What time is good?"

"Give me at least an hour. Oh. And we'll meet at the library."

Karla agreed to meet her there before flipping her phone closed.

Her stomach gave a little growl. Obviously her lunch hadn't been enough for her, but she just didn't really feel like eating at lunch time. The butterflies had made her feel too nausea. Now she needed to get something in her stomach or she really would get sick. So she decided to go to the kitchen to grab a snack.

Her mom was on the phone in the living room. She quickly grabbed a couple of cookies and soda and slipped back to her bedroom. She tried to settle her nerves by nibbling on the chocolate chip cookies.

Karla remembered the newspaper meeting for tomorrow. She almost forgot. She needed to let her mom know she'd be late coming home on Saturday. She really wanted to go to this newspaper meeting at the library.

But first she needed to change out of the skirt and shoes. She knew her mom would ask questions if she saw her dressed like this.

Leaving the sanctuary of her room, she checked to see if her mom was done on the phone. She found her already in the kitchen.

"Oh, yeah… Mom…In the morning, I'll be late. I decided to join the school newspaper, and I've to stop at the library Saturday morning, there is going to be a school newspaper meeting I've to go to."

"What do you mean – late?"

"Remember you said I could go to Carol's sleepover." Karla's stomach churned again, her mother better not change her mind now.

"Oh – right, about that – I don't think it is going to be a good idea. I think you should stay home, here with us."

Karla's heart sunk into her stomach. "NO. You said I could go and I told Carol you said I could go. So I'm going." She was not going to let her mom change her mind on her. Not now. This was not going to happen.

Her mom looked at her with narrowed eyes.

"You dare talk to me like that young miss?"

"But Mom… I didn't want to move here and now I've to make new friends. If I don't go now that I've told everyone I'm going… They'll laugh at me in school and call me a baby. Don't be doing this to me, 'cause I never wanted to move here in the first place. You're so not being fair to me."

Her mom was silent for a moment.

"But if you get into any trouble…" Her mom broke off and hesitated before continuing, "But yes, I'm glad you found something you like about this school. Newspaper, now that's something good for you. Just make sure you call me in the morning to let me know you made it to the newspaper meeting."

"I'll…"

Karla wasted no time. She had headed back into her room as quickly as she could before her mom started to change her mind again.

Back in her room she stopped to check nervously on her cell phone for any new messages. Nothing. She started packing her backpack.

The decision of what to wear was a hard choice to make. She shoved her clothes on her closet rack back and forth, looking for the perfect article. Not wanting to seem like she was too easy, she settled for a long-sleeved red top with a hood and a v-neckline.

Karla took the time to fold the top carefully to eliminate any wrinkles from forming, packing the top into the backpack. Carefully she packed her skirt too. She put the last article of clothing in the bag with her hair accessories and make-up piled on top and zipped the bag shut.

She thought about wearing her sneakers, but she decided on wearing the heels after all.

She checked one last time for any messages on her cell phone and stuffed the phone into the pocket on the outside of the backpack. Karla slung the bag over her shoulder and made her way past the kitchen.

She moved quickly by her mom her throat tightening up as she passed in fear. She was afraid her mom would change her mind again.

"I'm leaving now, mom."

"You be careful, you hear me…Remember, you can say no to friends…"

Her mom smiled as best she could. She gave in to trusting Karla, hoping she'd make good choices. She held her tongue as she watched Karla walk out the door.

# 24

KARLA HURRIED ALONG DOWN THE STREET, TRYING NOT TO RUN.
She was excited to be free to be with her friends.

The traffic was thick and backed up.

She stopped at the crosswalk and was annoyed by the light at the corner and the fact that these shoes were starting to hurt her feet. She began to wish she'd changed into her sneakers after all. Why's this light taking so long to change?

Finally, the light changed after what seemed like time standing still. Karla fought the urge to run. Her feet were actually killing her from the shoes causing her to walk slower anyway. Crossing the street, she headed as quickly as she could towards the library.

A passing mustang blared, bass pounding loudly from its speakers.

Karla hurried up the steps of the library when she saw Carol sitting there with her other friends. Hopefully, they hadn't been waiting long for her. She was so happy to see them, and she couldn't believe she was doing this.

"Glad you could make it," Carol greeted Karla.

Carol and her friends stood and began to move off the library steps almost before she reached the base of them. Karla could do anything but follow the girls.

She thought Carol had sounded a bit snotty. She wondered what her problem was. Ignore it she thought, maybe it was really nothing.

Walking down the street to Carol's house, they stopped on the way to chat with a couple of guys who graduated from school the previous year. Karla didn't know who they were, but she thought they looked cute.

"How much," one of the guys asked.

Carol put up four fingers and took the package from him. She quickly pocketed the object out of Karla's sight.

Karla thought she saw something in a bag, but she was just not sure about it.

"Have fun tonight," the other guy called after them.

The girls made their way back down the street from where they'd just come from.

She was not sure where they were going now. Karla followed closely behind. It was as though she were a little kid tagging along with the big kids, almost like they wanted to lose her or something.

She made sure she kept up with them. They weren't going to lose her; she'd make sure of that.

Carol turned down a side street. It was an area of town Karla hadn't been in yet. She was surprised to see the backside of the school grounds appear before them.

They walked across the soccer field and parking lot to the football field bleachers. Her feet were getting numb from her shoes. Karla took a seat on the bleacher behind Carol. Darcy and Maggie each sat beside Carol.

She was happy they'd decided to stop and watch the game. Her aching feet throbbed in her shoes. She wasn't going to say anything about it to them. She knew they'd just laugh at her for wearing such silly shoes to a sleepover and party. They went with the outfit she picked to wear to the party that was the only reason she'd worn them.

Karla watched the game. She needed to watch it for the school newspaper anyway. If only she'd brought her camera with her so she could've taken some photo shots of the plays.

She had a hard time making out what the plays were, and who were the players. At one point, she thought she saw Gerry, but she was not sure.

Carol, Darcy, and Maggie waved to their friends sitting nearby in the bleachers. Maggie pointed to the kicker and tried to say something about the player. Karla couldn't hear her well over the loud crowd.

A whistle blew during the last play. One of the football players jogged over to a fallen player on the ground. Apparently, he'd taken an extra-hard hit. Carol let out a sigh when the player finally stood up. She wondered if it was Heath. Karla couldn't tell from where she sat.

Marla and Jerra sat in the bleachers off to Karla's left. She wanted to wave to them, but they wouldn't look in her direction. The cold shoulder she was getting from Carol and her friends at this point, made her wish she was hanging with Marla and Jerra. At least they probably would've been talking to her.

While she watched the game, she began to daydream about Gerry. About what it'd be like to be with him. She was startled out of her dream by a horn blowing. This seemed to signal the end of the game. Karla squinted to see the scoreboard, but the setting sun was shining in her eyes.

"Who won," she asked Carol.

"We did, of course," Darcy answered.

"Oh...," Karla was not sure she liked Darcy. Her attitude was a bit off, but she was a little bit nicer than Maggie. Maybe she just doesn't like me, or she's in a bad mood, she thought to herself.

They sat on the bleachers, waiting for the crowd to pile off the field, the visitors leaving the field first. A tune was struck up by the home marching band performing in the middle of the field.

Carol jumped up off the bench first. Karla quickly picked up her bag. She wondered if she'd be ditched at any moment. Following the pack of girls off the grounds left Karla with a feeling of being ignored. She was beginning to have second thoughts about the evening again. Maybe this hadn't been such a good idea after all.

They again crossed back over the soccer field and parking lot, traveling in the same direction they'd come from. A red pickup truck caught Karla's eye. It was parked next to a dumpster in the alleyway. She heard someone yell from a doorway. They sounded angry. Quickening up her step, she stuck to Darcy's side like glue until they left the alleyway.

Main Street was still busy. The cars zoomed past them, only to slow down at the stoplight or come to a stop. Karla hadn't been in this area of downtown. Cool shops lined the street. She thought it was neat how they made the sidewalk out of red brick, but it was really hard to walk on in these shoes she was wearing. God. Her feet hurt.

Karla kept up as best as she could. Another side street appeared on their right. Carol turned down this road. She was so glad they were finally slowing down. She was not sure how much more her feet could take.

They were now on the street leading to Carol's house. Karla was still in tow. Apartment buildings lined the street. They all were old style townhouses, duplexes, and older apartment buildings. Each one was almost right on top of the other building. It appeared not one had much of a yard for young children to play in.

Three five or six-year-old girls played jump rope on the sidewalk. Carol and Darcy teased the girls making the girl jumping the rope miss. Another group of seven or eight-year-olds were playing hopscotch further down the sidewalk. Maggie kicked their stones off their spots.

Karla wondered how they could be so mean to these kids. They didn't do anything to them. Why could they not leave them alone? She thought about sticking up for them, but she knew she was outnumbered. So, she just stood back and watched, shaking her head the whole while.

Further down this street, Carol lived in a duplex with an old, rickety porch. Plastic patio furniture was set out on the porch.

They stepped up onto the porch. Almost immediately Karla saw that their favorite pastime was to call out to a friend or jeer an unknown pedestrian.

"Hey, Darren…you going tonight," Darcy called out to a passing car. The car stopped short and backed up. Darcy ran off the porch to chat with the driver. She hung on the front passenger window for a few minutes, and then stepped back finally, and the car pulled away.

They entered Carol's house. Karla couldn't believe the mess in the living room and the kitchen. She'd never been in a home so unkempt.

They ignored Carol's parents when they passed through the living room. Not one of them greeted either of the adults. Karla wanted to, but she held her tongue.

All four girls piled into Carol's bedroom. Karla followed them, setting her bag down on Carol's bedroom floor.

Carol's bedroom walls were lined with posters, mostly of guys on the beach, and a couple of them were of some white rapper. Karla had never heard of him.

She had a ratty old carpet on her bedroom floor. It looked like it needed to be vacuumed badly. There was a window which was almost the full length of the wall from the ceiling to the floor. It had an old sheet for a curtain.

The window looked out into what could be called a back yard. The view was of the apartment on the next street, just a stone throw away. They were all run down apartments too.

She stood and watched them at first, not sure what they were going to do next. So she waited until they began to change for the night's activities.

Karla pulled her top out of her backpack. She took off her top and started to put on the one from her bag.

"You're not gonna wear that, are you?" Carol asked her. "Here, wear one of mine…Gerry should really like this one on you."

Carol handed Karla a black, racy top from her closet with a very low-cut in the front. There were straps that went around the neck, exposing the back. It was a perfect match for the short skirt she brought with her, the one she wore to school today.

"Isn't that the top you got from the mall a couple of weeks ago?" Maggie asked. "The one you almost got caught with?"

Karla knew she'd feel funny wearing such a top, knowing now that most likely it was stolen, but she put it on anyway. Wanting to please her new-found friends, she admired it in the mirror.

"Oh…. So. What do you care," Carol snipped back, "Like you'd be able to fit in it. Look. See. It fits Karla perfectly…"

Carol put on a racy outfit too; and checked herself in her mirror. She appeared to be happy with how it fit. She then moved back over to where Karla stood, and began assisting her with the make-up when she needed help.

"You think he's gonna like this," Karla asked while checking herself out in the mirror.

"Oh, yeah, he's gonna love it," answered Darcy with a smile. She knew—just like Carol and Maggie knew—what kind of reaction Karla would get from Gerry by wearing such an outfit.

Carol opened her closet and began rummaging in the bottom of it. She found the bottle she'd stashed under her dirty clothes. Taking plastic disposable cups, she poured everyone a drink. She dropped something in each of the cups before handing them out.

Karla peered into her cup. She couldn't see what the item was. The soda was dark and fizzed. She put the cup to her lips and sipped. It seemed to taste tolerable. The liquid seemed to burn the back of her throat a bit.

"It's just a little something to help you relax," Carol reassured her. "Let's toast to a fun-filled evening."

Carol held up her glass for everyone to click.

Karla touched her cup against Carol's with the other girls. She was reluctant to drink the liquid, but it was what everyone else was doing. With the cup pressed to her lips, she tried to drink the liquid as fast as she could, the liquid burning the back of her throat as it went down.

Karla then found a place to sit. She sat on the bed and waited, listening while the girls began to talk about the volleyball meet coming up next week.

Pushing a pile of blankets up onto the pillows against the wall the bed was against, Carol took a spot on the bed behind Karla.

"I'm gonna fix your hair for you."

Carol took her brush and hair bands and changed Karla's hairstyle. When she was done, she held up a mirror for Karla's approval.

"Wow. That style looks great on you, Karla," Maggie giggled. Her eyes had a glassy appearance to them.

"Yeah, Carol. You really should be a hair dresser," Darcy agreed.

"I like it. Thanks Carol," Karla said while she looked at it in a hand held mirror. Her head was beginning to swim, but she was relaxed. Maybe she was just making something out of nothing when she believed they were going to ditch her earlier.

"Are we gonna go, or what?" Darcy impatiently asked.

Carol looked at the alarm clock.

"We're waiting a bit. We've to wait until 8:00—that's when Ian said to wait until. He wants to make sure his dad leaves first."

# 25

"WELL, IT IS ALMOST TIME…," DARCY GIGGLED. "WE CAN WALK slow, I just want to get going. I can't wait to see Darren."

"Yeah, we all know why you can't wait to see Darren," Maggie teased her. "We all know what you're gonna be doing with him."

"Sh… You don't have to tell the world," Darcy laughed.

"You guys gonna get married when you're done with school," Carol asked.

"Who knows? Maybe sooner," Darcy bragged.

"Why?," Karla asked, more confident, even though her mind was nothing but fog. The room seemed to move in the opposite direction she moved in. God. How weird, I wonder if this is how mom feels when she drinks stuff like this? She fought to keep her focus on Darcy after she realized her mind was wandering.

"Oh…I might be…you know…," Darcy giggled.

"And you're going to a party," Karla asked.

"Oh, it is only gonna be this one time," Darcy giggled. "And I can't be that far along, so it can't do too much damage."

"I think we can go now," announced Carol and she led them out of the bedroom.

Karla was a little worried about leaving her bag behind, but she did leave it. She left her cell phone too. She was afraid she'd lose it at the party. She was sure it'd be safe there.

They passed Carol's parents sitting in the living room.

"You be home by midnight," Carol's dad called out from behind his newspaper. He'd a can of beer on the table beside him.

Carol's mom was asleep on the coach. She didn't even stir. Beer cans line the coffee table in front of her.

"Okay, Dad," she replied giggling. Carol shut the front door behind them as they made their way off the porch and on to the party.

"I thought Gerry was picking us up," Karla said to Carol. Never ever having had any alcohol before, she didn't know what a fizz-maker was but it sure made her feel good. Even her feet didn't hurt her anymore. Karla stifled a giggle.

"We can walk. I saw him right after school, and he said he'd meet us there…said he'd some stuff to do first."

"Oh…," Karla said. It appeared as though she were as light as a feather. She wondered if they were almost there yet. She had a hard time focusing her eyes. Everything was so blurry.

Loud music came from a building up ahead of them. Karla stumbled a bit, and Carol grabbed her arm, steadying her. Both girls began to giggle.

The girls walked up the steps to Ian's house. A two story single family house, it was five houses down on a side street off of the Main Street. A bunch of cars were parked along the sidewalk and in the driveway.

Gerry and his buddies were standing on the steps smoking, waiting for the girls. Darkness caused the streetlights to come on. The porch light was on. Karla stopped at Gerry's side and took the bottle he offered to her, drinking a swig. The liquid burned the back of her throat again.

He pulled the bottle away from her, laughing. "Hey, girl, slow down. You don't have to drink it so fast."

Karla handed the bottle back to Gerry, while wiping her mouth with the back of her hand. "Here, you want some more," Karla let out a giggle—she couldn't help it.

"Na…I'm gonna get another one. You can have that one."

Karla took another sip of the bottle. "What's this stuff, anyway," She held out the bottle, trying to get a better look at the label.

"Mark's Lemonade," Gerry replied, "…Thought you might like it."

"It tastes good."

Karla moved closer to Gerry.

"Nice outfit. I like it."

He seemed to tilt his head a bit.

Karla giggled again, "Thanks. I'm glad you like it."

Gerry moved closer to Karla. The music was loud. She could barely hear him when he spoke.

"Let's go somewhere where we can be alone, and maybe talk."

He offered his hand to her.

Karla accepted it. She let him lead her into the house. He stopped to greet his friends and pick up another bottle.

Maggie spied them as they came close to the table where the drinks were setting out for those to take. She made sure she uncapped the bottle first before she handed it to Gerry to take. Her hand casually passed over the open top of the bottle.

"Wow. She looks great," Heath said giving his approval.

"We're going up stairs for a bit," Gerry announced.

Karla giggled. The guys were all staring at her. She was not used to being the center of attention. God, look at the way they're looking at me. I must really look "great."

She thought to herself.

She let Gerry lead her up the stairs. He motioned her to enter a large bedroom with a big bed. Karla stepped into the room. Gerry quickly closed the door behind them.

"There, that's better."

Gerry smiled. The door blocked out the blaring music from the floor below.

Karla started to look around the room. She began to wonder who this bedroom belonged to. She noticed a dresser with a lot of stuff on it. A small electric burner stood in the mess on the dresser. She thought it was weird; they seemed to cook food in their room. Karla giggled.

"Karla, come sit over here with me."

Gerry motioned to a spot next to him on the bed.

Karla sat down on the bed, it was good to sit down—the room spun every time she moved.

"Are you done with your drink," Gerry asked.

Karla didn't remember finishing the drink. She shook the bottle to find it was empty.

"I guess so."

"Here, I got you another one," Gerry handed her the one he'd taken from Maggie. It was almost full.

"What're you gonna drink," Karla asked.

He pulled a beer from a cooler hidden under the bed.

"See? I'm all set."

Karla giggled.

"I guess you are. How many do you have in there?"

"Enough for now," Gerry popped the top off the beer can.

"Wanna try some of this?"

He offered the can to her.

Karla took a sip.

"Yuck. I'll stick with the lemonade."

She handed the can back to him.

Gerry laughed.

"I thought so. Most girls don't like it."

Karla took a long drink of her lemonade. She needed to get rid of the bitter taste of the beer. The lemonade went down smoother. She no longer noticed the burning sensation in the back of her throat.

Gerry reached out and gently took the bottle from her, setting it down on the night stand next to the bed.

"God, you look so good. Can I kiss you?"

Karla couldn't help but giggle.

"Of course you can, silly."

She let him pull her into his arms. Oh my God. She thought. This is my first kiss. I hope I do this right. His smooth lips against hers, she let him pull her closer. His tongue entered her mouth—this startled her.

He slowly, gently directed her to lie down on the bed. Her body responded in ways she didn't know was possible, surprising her. She couldn't resist. The room spun once again from the sudden movement.

Karla was nervous. She'd never been with a guy before. His lips move to her neck making her giggle. Her body continued to respond to his touches making her feel funny in places she never knew existed, it excited her.

While Gerry began to explore her body with his hands, Karla liked his touches. She gasped when he untied the strings of her top, sliding it down to her stomach, exposing her breasts.

She wasn't sure where this was all going. Something nagged the back of her mind. It must've been something she'd read or heard before. Karla wanted to tell Gerry to stop, but she didn't want him to stop. She wondered what he was doing to her.

Her head swam even more. She thought she heard a humming sound in her ears. Her vision twisted in weird ways.

Gerry kissed her some more, making his way further down her body with his lips and slowly undressing her. Karla felt helpless. She wondered how she could get him to stop. Did she really want him to stop? Not really. She really loved what he was doing to her. It was so right.

Karla's breathing became heavy when he shifted his body on top of hers, pushing her legs apart, and his groin pushed into her pelvis. She couldn't resist. She couldn't believe what he was doing to her. She wondered why her vision was so weird?

She tried to move her arm. It seemed too heavy to lift when she tried to push Gerry off her, but she couldn't find the strength. She tried to tell him, "No, don't do that," but the words wouldn't come from her lips. Her breathing was very heavy. Her face was hot, as though it were a hundred degrees in the room. Why was it so hot, she wondered?

Karla let out a gasp when he slipped himself inside her. She wanted to scream no, and struggled under him weakly. Her self-control was completely gone.

She was excited and confused, wondering why she was letting him do this to her. It was only their first date. But she loved it, he made her feel so good. And, why was she suddenly so thirsty?

The door burst open with no warning. Heath, Justin, Kyle, and Mitch flooded into the room, laughing.

"All right, man. Time's up. Our turn," Justin laughed. "Hope you saved some for us."

Karla wanted to scream. Gerry removed himself from her. She wanted to scream, really, really scream. God. No. Help. Something was preventing Karla from calling out. She didn't know if it was the alcohol, or what was wrong with her. She was panic-stricken when the four boys approached her as she lay helpless on the bed.

The room went dark.

# 26

"GOD, CAN YOU BELIEVE THOSE GUYS," DEVIN SIPPED HIS BEER. HE took a toke of the joint and passed it on to the next person.

"Yeah, man. They're gonna get their asses caught one of these days," Sean accepted the joint. He took a toke of it too and passed it on.

Carol overheard them talking. The smell of the pot had floated across the room to her. She wanted a hit of it. Moving across the room through the crowd, she found a place in the group next to Sean. She was just in time for a turn for a hit.

"That girl is probably gonna be a mess in the morning."

Devin lifted his can to his lips again.

"What girl," Carol squeaked.

"The girl Gerry took upstairs," Ian piped in. He accepted the joint from Carol.

"I think she's one of your new friends."

Sean held out his hand, waiting for Devin to pass the joint to him.

"What did he do to her," Maggie brought Carol another cooler and sat down on the floor beside Carol. She really wanted to know if that knew girl was going to get what was coming to her. Take her man from her; no one takes her man from her.

Maggie reached into her pocket to pull out another joint. Lighting it, she took a hit and passed it to Carol.

"Um, maybe you shouldn't know," replied Sean as he lifted his can to his lips.

"Now I want to know."

Carol glared at Sean.

"Carol, don't tell me you don't know the type of guy Gerry is. You've known him for how many years," Ian said while took a hit off the joint.

"That don't mean anything," Carol said. "What did he do that's so bad? Why did you say she'd probably be messed up in the morning? He's just screwing her. Right?"

"Well, put it this way: What happens when a guy puts some G in your drink," Ian asked.

"Yeah," Sean said, "And the four of them went up to help Gerry finish. They said he'd been up there too long, and he'd to share the fun." He took another hit of the joint.

"What four? Oh my God, you don't mean Heath too?"

This was bull, there was no way Carol was going to listen to anyone say stuff like that about her guy. But then what was this talk about the G?

Carol asked, "You said he gave her G?"

Four guys jogged down the stairs each one laughing. Heath was in the middle of the pack. Carol ran to the foot of the stairs and caught Heath by the arm. Drawing her arm back, she smacked Heath across the face.

"Where's Karla," she screamed at him.

"She fell asleep on Gerry," Heath snickered. He rubbed the side of his face, "What the hell was that for?"

Carol shoved Heath out of her way. "The plan was that only Gerry was going to mess with her, not the rest of you. You bastards!"

She stormed up the stairs to check on her friend. She found her out cold, and hot to touch. Grabbing Karla's arms, she dragged her to the shower. "Oh my God, Karla...," she whispered, "I'm so sorry...I didn't know he was gonna give you G."

Carol feared the worst as she struggled with Karla's limp body. It was just too limp to get her into the shower.

The front door slammed. Carol could hear yelling outside the house. The voices were muffled. She couldn't make out what they were saying.

"Help, somebody," she screamed, "Help me get her into the shower."

Ian ran up the stairs to Carol's aid. "What's some' matter?"

"I think she OD'ed on ecstasy, help me," Carol screamed frantically, trying to drag her friend to the shower.

Ian helped Carol put Karla into the shower, turning the cold water on her. Karla didn't respond.

"What're we gonna do?" Carol asked. She didn't know what she was freakin' gonna do if she couldn't get Karla to come around.

"We've to think of something," Ian tried smacking Karla several times on her cheek—no response.

"We've to get help, or she'll die," Carol screamed.

The yelling outdoors grew louder. Carol heard someone yell, "Pigs."

A car started up, loudly revving its motor. The car doors slammed. It took off with screeching tires.

Police cars pulled up out front with blue lights flashing. The light flashed the walls with color from the upstairs window. One of the neighbors must've called the cops on them for playing the music too loud.

Carol and Ian knew they couldn't run like the rest of their friends had when the blue lights drove down the street. They stayed with Karla as the cops entered the house. The front door had been left open when the last kid sprinted away down the street, leaving Carol, Ian, and Karla alone in the house.

Carol didn't care about what was about to happen. They could arrest her if they wanted. She was more afraid of what was happening to Karla, fearing Karla was about to die—if she hadn't already.

"Help, please help us. Up here. Quick. Help. My friend is going to die…Help."

The officers responded quickly to find them upstairs with Karla in the shower. She was still not responding.

"This is K6149; we need medical assistance at 49 Breen Crest Drive. We've a possible drug overdose."

The officer addressed Carol: "I'm Officer James. What's your friend's name?"

He quickly snapped on the hallway light.

"Her name is Karla, Karla Centon."

"What's your name?"

Carol tried to see over the officer's shoulder while another officer checked to see if Karla still had a pulse.

"I got a pulse. It is weak, though."

"Oh my God… Karla, please wake up, please," Carol pleaded. She forgot all about being questioned by the officer.

"You need to step over here, out-of-the-way. You'll be of no help to her if you're in the way."

Officer James reached out and grabbed Carol by the arm, leading her away from the bathroom.

"What's your name? I need to see some ID."

"Carol," she said excitedly, "My name is Carol Bower. Oh my God. Is she gonna be all right?"

A flashing red light flickered in the bedroom window. The paramedics had arrived. Two more officers escorted the paramedics up the stairs to tend to Karla.

"Is she gonna be okay," Carol asked the paramedics.

"They won't know until they take your friend to the hospital."

Officer James escorted Carol into the bedroom Karla and Gerry had occupied.

"Can you tell me what happened, Carol? Do you know what she took, or what she drank?"

The dresser with the paraphernalia and clutter caught her eye. Oh God, not this room. Shit.

"Carol, do you've any ID on you? Do you live here?"

Officer James noticed Carol was staring at the items on the dresser.

"Who does this room belong to? Do you know?"

He reached into his pocket, pulled out a penlight, and flashed it before Carol's eyes.

The sight of the cooking burner made Carol's heart skip a beat. Oh no. Where's Ian, she wondered.

Looking out the bedroom door, she was able to see into the bedroom across the hallway. Ian stood with his hands behind his back. Another officer searched Ian and placed handcuffs on him.

"I don't have any ID on me. I left it at home," Carol said quickly.

"So, you don't live here," Officer James asked again. He began to look over the items on the dresser.

Carol knew she was about to be arrested. She heard the officer call on his radio for assistance from a female officer. The female officer quickly appeared in the room. Carol was sure she'd been waiting downstairs.

"Carol, my name is Theresa; I'm going to need to search you. Do you've anything on you that you shouldn't have? Like any weapons or drugs, or maybe anything sharp that I can get stuck by," Officer Theresa directed Carol to face the wall. She kicked her legs apart.

Carol's arms were yanked behind her as she shook her head no.

No, this wasn't happening to her, and no she didn't have anything sharp or otherwise on her person.

Her face was shoved up against the wall. The sharp pain made her gasp when her hair was used to steer her closer against the wall. Cold cuffs were suddenly snapped tightly on her wrists.

"I don't live here," Carol pleaded, "I don't have any weapons in my pockets."

"What about anything else? Will I get stuck by a needle if I reach into your pockets? I don't want to get stuck by anything," Officer Theresa began to search Carol's upper body after Carol shook her head no one more time.

"No... I don't have anything in my pockets."

"What do we've here," Officer Theresa pulled a small bag from Carol's pocket. "What's this stuff, Carol? Is it what I think it is?"

She held up the bag for Carol to see.

"I don't know…I don't remember putting that there," Carol stammered.

"Looks like a bag of rock to me. Doesn't it look like that to you?"

Theresa placed the bag into some sort of special bag marked Evidence.

"And you don't remember putting it into your pocket? I don't know, Carol. Why don't you try to tell me the truth? I'll give you just one chance to make this right."

"Yes. It is rock. Am I going to jail? Is my friend going to be all right?" Carol asked as she tried to change the subject. She wanted to pull away when Officer Theresa pat her down the rest of the way, ending with her legs last.

"Carol, I need you to take off your shoes," she instructed.

Carol kicked off her shoes. The cuffs were digging into her wrists.

"Do these really need to be so tight," she complained.

"You can take a seat right there on the floor."

Officer Theresa pointed to a spot on the hallway floor.

Carol bit her lip, trying to hold back tears. She knew her folk were going to be pissed. Dropping to the floor, she watched the officer join Officer James next to the dresser.

"So, Carol, tell me, who does this room belong too," Officer James asked again.

"I don't live here," Carol said defensively. She looked around to see where Ian was, but he was nowhere in sight.

"Then where do you live, Carol," Officer Theresa asked while looking over the paraphernalia on the dresser. "We'll need to contact someone—who do we contact for you?"

"How old are you, Carol," Officer James asked. He began to write things down on a pad of paper.

"I live at 292 Kemper Street with my parents Doug and Ellen Bower. I'm six-teen," Carol blurted out. She'd been trying to hold back the tears the whole time she was being searched. Now she couldn't hold them back anymore—her lip began to tremble.

The paramedics carried Karla down the stairs on the gurney. Carol's stomach knotted up at the sight. Oh, God. Help her.

Officer James and Theresa escorted Carol down the stairs behind the paramedics and out of the house. The cold steel cuffs gripping her wrists bit into her skin. She began again thinking of her parents. Oh, God, they're gonna be pissed... God, I hope Karla is gonna be all right.

Officer Theresa opened the right-side rear passenger door on the police cruiser.

"Carol, I need you to bend a bit so you don't bang your head."

Putting her hand on top of Carol's head, she guided her into the car.

Ian was already sitting in the backseat of the car. Carol could see he didn't look happy. She understood why. Trying to lean back in the car, her bound arms hurt from the position they were in.

# 27

"WHY DID YOU GIVE HER THAT STUFF," IAN ASKED AS HE GLARED AT Carol sitting next to him in the backseat.

"What stuff," Carol asked innocently.

"You know, the X," Ian hissed.

"I don't know what you're talking' about."

Carol looked out the window toward the ambulance. The paramedics were putting Karla in the back, shutting the doors—she was out of sight again.

"Then how'd you know she was OD'ing on X?"

Ian leaned forward, trying to relieve the pressure on his arms.

"I did," asked Carol as she played innocent.

"Yeah…when you ran upstairs to find Karla…you were screaming," Ian said while he rocked side to side.

"Oh, I guess it was something Sean said just before Heath came down the stairs."

Carol looked away and out her window again.

"My folks are gonna be pissed when the cops call them."

She saw the officers approaching the car.

"I hope Karla is gonna be okay."

"I bet mine will be pissed too when he gets the call to come pick me up at the station."

Ian tried to turn his body off to the side, leaning against the door.

Carol's door opened. Officer James stood outside the door.

"I need to inform both of you of your right to stay silent. You've the right to have an attorney present during questioning. If you can't afford one, then one will be assigned to you. Do you understand your rights?" he asked, addressing Carol and Ian together.

"We're being arrested," Carol blurted.

"I didn't do anything," Ian protested, "You can't arrest me. I'm under eighteen."

"What're you arresting us for," Carol demanded.

"Look, there is very strong evidence of underage drinking going on here tonight, and we've found a substantial stash of drugs on the premises," Officer James replied.

"Your friend is in the middle of a drug overdose, and you're trying to say you didn't have a thing to do with it," Officer Theresa inquired.

"We're now going to take you both down to the station, and you'll be processed and wait to go before the judge," Officer James explained, "Your parents will be contacted."

"What's gonna happen to Karla," Carol asked. "Is she gonna be all right?"

"Your friend is being taken to Kendall County Hospital. Hopefully, she'll arrive in time to have her stomach pumped. You need to start praying for her. Hopefully, it isn't too late. If she doesn't get medical attention in time, then she may die."

Officer James took the driver seat. Theresa sat beside him in the passenger seat. Carol head swam when the car lurched forward. It traveled down the street, taking a right-hand turn at the stop sign, on to the main street. The police station was on the other side of town.

They turned off of Main Street onto a by-pass, to get to the other side of town. Carol watched out her car window while occasionally glancing to her left out Ian's window.

# 28

SUDDENLY, THE CAR SLOWED DOWN TO A CRAWL, COMING TO A brief stop. Red lights flashed ahead.

"Oh my God...Is that Gerry's car?"

Carol leaned forward in her seat to get a better view out Ian's window. She could see fire trucks arriving. Firemen were pulling hoses from the trucks toward the car.

"Shit. It is Gerry's car."

Ian gawked out his window at the car resting on its roof.

Flames circled around the outside of the car. A lone figure stood holding some sort of extinguisher beside one of the fire trucks. He was speaking to one of the firemen and pointing toward the car.

A tractor trailer truck was off the curb, twisted on its side.

Two bodies lay in the street, not moving.

The firemen ran from their truck toward the car, toward the driver-side. They were carrying some sort of gadget. The man who'd been pointing toward the car began trying to pull the driver-side door open. It didn't seem to budge.

One of the firemen started up the gadget, it sounded like a chainsaw.

"Do you think they're going to be okay?" Carol asked.

"Shit. That looks bad, real bad," Ian replied.

"Is there any way we can find out if those guys in that car are all right?" Carol asked the officers.

"Nope," Officer Theresa replied. "You're gonna have to wait it out. Ask your parents when they come down to the station."

The police car passed an ambulance on its way to the accident. Its siren was blaring, and its lights were flashing. This was then followed by another ambulance traveling in the same direction.

"It's too bad that things like this happen when kids start holding drinking parties," Officer James stated.

"Yeah," Officer Theresa agreed. "They took a fun Friday night, and added drugs and alcohol. It didn't take long for it to turn into a total disaster for themselves and their friends."

The police car picked speed back up as they left the crash scene. They were at the police station before Carol knew it. She could only think about Karla and Gerry.

The buzz in her head began to dull. A throbbing headache grew between her eyes. She began to think more about how pissed her folks were gonna be with her.

Officer Theresa opened Carol's door and pulled her out of the car. When she grabbed a hold of Carol's shirt, Carol clinched her teeth. She hated being treated like an animal.

She was then led into the station. It was late. Carol could see the time on the clock on the wall. It was now half-past eleven. She knew her folks were gonna be more than pissed. She was gonna be grounded.

Officer Theresa left Carol to sit on a bench to wait. Her head was starting to pound. Why did she choose to drink those wine coolers, they gave her a headache every time.

After twenty minutes went by, Officer Theresa returned to Carol. She'd a pad and pen in her hand. "Carol, what's your home phone number? So I can call your parents to come get you."

Carol wondered what'd happen if she didn't give the officer her phone number. "What happens if I don't have a home phone number?"

"Well then, we would have to go in person to your home and notify your parents that we've got you in custody," Officer Theresa informed her. "We can do it either way. Which way do you want your parents notified?"

"521-8004," Carol answered. She didn't like the thought of the police showing up at her home.

"Now see, wasn't that easy," Officer Theresa jotted down the number on her pad. "I'll go call them for you."

Another half-an hour passed. Carol still sat on the bench. The handcuffs were still on her wrists. She slumped forward on the bench. The cuffs were tight enough, she was afraid if she put any more pressure on them, they'd tighten even more.

She could see the traffic walking into the station from where she sat. People would come into the station and walk past the door in front of her, on their way to the desk.

Her dad finally showed up. He looked like he'd thrown his clothes on real quick. He walked right past the door to the room in which she sat. He never noticed her sitting there.

A few minutes later, Officer Theresa returned, "Your Dad is here to take you home. You'll receive a summons in the mail to appear in court."

She undid the cuffs behind Carol's back.

Carol looked up to see her dad standing there before her. He looked pissed. She rubbed her wrists where the cuffs had dug into them.

"Let's go young lady," Her dad ordered. "Thanks again Officer."

She followed her dad out to the car. She was sure she'd be grounded. This was the first time she'd ever been caught by the law.

In the car, they rode home mostly in silence. Just before they pulled onto their street, her dad broke the silence. "I not only got a call from the police tonight, but I also got a call from a very hysteric Mrs. Centon. I guess her daughter is a friend of yours?"

Carol didn't answer right away. She knew he was waiting for some sort of reply. They pulled up in front of their house. She started to put her hand on the doorknob.

"Where do you think you're going, young lady," his voice boomed. It shook a nerve deep inside her. He only spoke to her like this when she really did something wrong. Like really bad, wrong.

"I'm waiting for an answer."

"Yes. Her daughter Karla was supposed to sleepover here tonight. We were going to go to the movies, but these guys saw us on our way there and asked us to come over to their place and watch movies with them. We figured we could save a few bucks, with free movie and popcorn. We never expected there to be stuff going on there. Honest Dad."

"Well, that stuff may have cost your friend her life tonight. They weren't sure if she was going to pull through," her dad lectured. "I think it is time you started to find new friends. I'm not going to stand for this sort of stuff."

"All right Dad, I'll break up with Heath. He's a jerk anyway," Carol bargained.

"Well that's a start."

He opened his car door, signaling the lecture was over for now.

"Oh, by the way, your mom doesn't know about this. Okay? She doesn't need to know for now."

Carol was relieved, "Okay, thanks Dad."

She followed her dad into the house and went right to her bedroom. Karla's bag was still on her bedroom floor right where she'd left it. Carol pushed it off to the side of her room. She'd have to find a way to return it to her home sometime soon, but not now.

She rummaged in her closet. The liquor bottle was gone. Her dad must've gone looking and found it while she sat at the police station.

She shoved the fallen belongings back into her closet and looked across her room. The floor board looked like it was still in the same state she'd left it in. Maybe her stuff was still there. She quietly walked across her room and slipped the short floor board up from its hole. Underneath was her stuff. She smiled. At least it was still there.

She picked up one of the small baggies containing the powder substance. She smiled again. She'd her stuff and that was all that mattered to her right now.

# 29

THE NEXT DAY, CAROL SLIPPED OUT THE DOOR BEFORE HER MOM
or dad woke. They were heavy late sleepers. She was sure she'd be able to return home
before they woke up.

She walked a block up the street. She needed to see if Darcy was home. Maybe
she heard something about the accident last night.

Darcy lived in an old gray apartment building with her mom. They lived on the
third floor. The rundown apartment building had several families living in it. You
could always hear someone's baby crying somewhere in the building.

Carol walked in the open door of the building and climbed the flight of stairs
up to the third floor. Darcy lived in apartment nine, Carol told herself. She stopped in
front of the door and knocked lightly.

She heard a muffled noise coming from inside the apartment. A latch was pulled
back. The door opened, and a little girl peeked out the crack, "Who you?"

"HI Amber… It's me Carol. Is Darcy home," she asked the little girl. She was
Darcy's niece. Her sister had lost custody of her a year ago, when she got busted for
doing tricks for drugs. Now Darcy's mom had her. She was not sure if Darcy's sister
would ever get Amber back. So sad she thought.

"Yeah, DARCY, Carol is here."

She swung the door open wide and let Carol inside. Carol had to shut the door
closed behind her. Amber had run off to find Darcy.

"Carol. Wha 'cha want," Darcy asked. She was still in her PJ's. Her hair still un-
combed.

"Did I wake you up," Carol chuckled.

Darcy led Carol into the kitchen and took a seat at the rickety kitchen table.
Holding her head in her hands she asked, "What gave you that idea?"

"Nothing… Hey did you hear anything about a car accident last night?"

"Um… No… Why," she asked as she sat back in her chair.

"Cause I heard there was some sort of accident last night. It sounded like it as

Gerry's car."

"Oh... Really...Wow. No I haven't heard anything. Did you try calling Heath?"

"No. And I'm not going to either. I'm breaking up with him."

Darcy decided to get herself a cup of yesterday's coffee. She poured it out of the coffee pot sitting on the counter and put it in the microwave to warm up. "Want some?"

Carol shook her head no.

"Why are you breaking up with him?"

She waited for the microwave to go beep and returned to the table with her coffee.

"Black coffee is the best you know."

"Oh we'd a fight last night. That's all. I don't want to talk about it."

Amber ran into the kitchen.

"Darcy the TV says car crash."

Carol and Darcy looked at each other. They followed Amber into the living room. Her cartoons were now replaced with some breaking news. The news camera showed the car after the driver-side door was ripped off. Apparently the news crew was reporting that the jaws of life were used last night to save the driver, who was trapped inside the car.

Two other passengers were airlifted to a trauma hospital in another city nearby. But no names were released at this time.

Carol sat down hard on the sofa. She knew that car. She'd ridden in it to school many times.

Now there was a big hole in the windshield. Oh my God. She wondered who the passengers were.

The news telecast changed. It moved on to an arrest that'd taken place last night. Ian's photo flashed across the screen along with his dad's photo. Oh my God. Not Ian, she thought. Damn, what's happening to her friends, and why did Ian's dad get arrested, she wondered.

"I got to go. Call me if you hear anything."

"Yup..."

Carol left Darcy's apartment in a hurry. The photo of the car wreck left her shaken. She hurried back home, making it in the door before her parents woke up.

She waited for the phone to ring. But it never did. She'd a feeling she'd have to wait until Monday before she heard anything about the car accident.

She sat in her room and stared at Karla's backpack and wondered if this party had been really worth it. Guilt was now eating her up inside, for being a part of setting Karla up for what she now faced.

She'd to find a way to make things up to Karla. Somehow make things right, but how?

Carol spent the rest of the day holed up in her room. It seemed as if her mom had no idea what'd taken place the night before. It was best this way. She was not in the mood for a shouting match with her today. Not after seeing the accident on TV.

There still was no word from Heath. Carol feared the worst. If he died right after she gave him, the-you-no-good smack, she wasn't sure how she'd be able to live with herself.

By two in the afternoon, a loud rap sounded on the front door. Carol could hear it from her room. She cracked open her door just enough to where she could peer out and see vague images of whoever stood at the door, and could barely making out the sound of their voices.

"Hi, we're with the Brantwood Police. Is your daughter home? We've a few questions to ask her about last night."

"What about," Carol's Mom inquired.

Carol could now see Officer Theresa and Officer James stood talking to her mom in the living room. Her dad came out of the kitchen carrying two beers. He held one out to her mom.

"Carol is in her room doing homework. Is she in trouble for something?"

"No, we just have some questions to ask her about her friend, Karla," Officer James stated.

"Carol...," Her dad called.

Carol walked slowly into the living room. She immediately recognized the two officers from last night.

"What," Carol asked. She tried to put on an air of being in the middle of her homework.

Carol saw her mom look at her reproachfully. She was thankful to Officer James taking her mom and dad off to the kitchen giving Carol privacy with the other officer.

"Carol, your friend Karla was in bad shape when she got to the hospital. It was a good thing you told us about her taking X. The doctors were able to treat her. They also discovered she'd ingested another substance. I was wondering if you might know how she came about this other substance," Theresa paused before continuing, "her clothes were also ripped in a certain way, indicating rape. We'd her tested for rape. What I need to know is do you know who the boys were?"

Carol looked toward the kitchen to make sure her parents weren't in earshot.

"So she's going to be all right?"

"Yes, as far as we can tell at this time. Did you know the other substance was G? She could've died. And what those boys did to her, you call them friends? What happened to her could've happened to you."

"She took G," Carol asked bewildered.

"Yes and when this is mixed with alcohol and X it can be very fatal."

Carol mouthed a big "O".

"You need to tell me who those boys are. Just because a person uses drugs, isn't all right for anyone to rape someone."

After biting her tongue for a moment, Carol gave in. "It was the boys in the car wreck we passed last night."

There she blurted it out. Now everyone would know by Monday morning, she was a snitch. Why should she cover Heath's back anyway? He shouldn't have been one of the guys who'd gone up to that room. And Gerry, he used her, that jerk.

"Thank you, Carol that was what we thought. Thanks for your cooperation."
Theresa closed up her pad of paper.

Carol quickly asked, "The boys… in the wreck …were they all right? I'ven't heard anything."

"They sustained severe injuries, but they lived. It was a miracle for them. They're currently in critical condition. You'll need to contact their families for a more current update."

Theresa turned toward her partner coming out of the kitchen followed by Carol's parents.

"We're done here. Thank you again for your cooperation."

After the officers left, her dad asked, "Is everything okay?"

"Yup, I've to go back to my homework."

With that Carol went back to her refuge of a room.

She slumped against her bed. Carol couldn't believe she'd just ratted out her friends. What the hell was she thinking? It'll be all around school before long, how she turned into a snitch. Maybe no one would know. She'd just have to be careful no one found out who the snitch was.

Carol knew what happened to snitches. And it was not good. She could take care of herself, but what if they all came after her. Well she'd have to worry about that later. Now was the time for a good binge.

She grabbed the bottle stashed under her bed. Maybe she could forget all about this weekend with just a little bit of help.

# 30

MR. CENTON WAITED OUTSIDE OF THE EMERGENCY ROOM. HE'D been waiting almost a half an hour since Karla was brought in. The police had spoken to him as soon as he'd arrived, telling him about what'd taken place. His wife hadn't arrived yet and wouldn't be there for another fifteen minutes.

After a brief discussion with the police officers, he asked them not to say a word about any of this to Karla's mom when she arrived. The police agreed after he explained Karla's tension plagued relationship with her mother. They agreed she wouldn't be of any great support for Karla and left the hospital before Mrs. Centon arrived.

\*\*\*

Karla woke to the sound of her parents voices. They were arguing as quietly as they could. This proved to be a very difficult task for either of them. Their voices slowly began to rise, thus waking Karla. She pretended to remain sleeping while she listened to their conversation.

"I knew, I just knew, I shouldn't have let her go out last night," Karla's mom sputtered.

"There was no way of knowing," Her dad argued, "This is what comes about when you don't let her learn on her own, how to make new friends. She's never going to learn who to trust and who not to trust. You just can't go on protecting her for the rest of her life."

"Protecting her from whom," Mrs. Centon stammered, "From herself. She used poor judgment. This should never have happened. And, I didn't protect her. I let her go and look what she went and did."

"There you go again, blaming Karla. If you'd been a proper mother, maybe, just maybe, she would've told you more about Carol in the first place."

"What do you mean, a proper mother? I'm a damn good mother. I've always been there for Karla. How dare you say I'm not a proper mother, look at you, you're never around."

"That's because of you."

"What do you mean, because of me?"

"You stay home and drink all day while I've to work two jobs just to support your ass."

"How dare you talk to me that way? And, I don't drink all day."

"If you'd been a proper mother, you would've gone out and gotten a job like me. Maybe, we wouldn't have lost our house."

"Oh. So now it is my fault that the bank foreclosed on our house."

"I guess I'm blaming you. If we hadn't lost our house, we'd never have had to move to Brantwood and Karla would never have been with that girl."

Karla couldn't stand it anymore. "Mom, Dad, why are you fighting again? What happened? Where am I?"

Mrs. Centon blurted angrily, "You're in the hospital. You almost died."

Karla shifted up in the bed. She couldn't believe what her mother just said. In fact, she couldn't remember anything. No matter how hard she tried, she could only remember the football game and going to Carol's house after the game. Nothing else, "Died, How?"

"Apparently, Miss, you and your supposedly friend Carol went to the movies with a bunch of other girls. Carol's dad said something about you and these girls met some boys at the theater and were invited back to one of their houses to watch movies there instead," Mr. Centon explained.

"They drugged you," Mrs. Centon added, "And gave you alcohol to drink."

"Huh? I don't know what you're talking about, Mom. Why'd I drink alcohol? I don't even like the stuff."

"Laurette, the doctor said this might happen. I'll be right back, I'm going to go find her and let her know Karla is awake."

After several uncomfortable moments being alone in the room with her mother, Mr. Centon returned with the Doctor.

"Hi Karla, it is good to see you're awake." The doctor then turned to Karla's parents and asked them to leave the room while she examined Karla in private.

The doctor continued speaking to Karla as soon as they were alone. "Your Dad informed me that you can't remember anything that happened. Can you tell me what you do remember?"

Karla racked her brain before answering, but she couldn't jog her memory in any way. "I only remember meeting with Carol and going to the football game at school and then going to Carol's house afterwards."

"Well apparently you were drugged last night and had been drinking. You were in the middle of a drug overdose when they brought you into the emergency room." The doctor paused before continuing. "The clothes we took off you were slightly torn and there is reason to believe you may have been a victim of a date rape drug. This is apparent due to the fact you can't remember anything about the incident.

I'd like permission to do a rape test on you, at the request of your Dad. He specifically mentioned to me, not to say anything about any of this to your Mom. Will you let me do the test?"

Karla couldn't believe what she was hearing. Her, a victim of rape, she couldn't remember anything. Who could've done such a thing to her? Did she even see Gerry last night? Why couldn't she remember anything?

"You won't tell my Mom about any of this?"

"No. Your Dad already told me about your relationship with your Mother. I promise I won't say a word about any of this to your Mom."

Karla agreed to let the doctor do her thing. One of the procedures was a pap smear. This was Karla's first one, and she found it an uncomfortable experience.

Afterwards, the doctor told Karla there was some trauma to her body indicating that she may have been raped. But it may be hard to prove in court. A sample from the examination was being submitted for testing, and they'd know about the results soon. They were also checking her to make sure she was not pregnant.

Karla couldn't believe what she was hearing. Did she really have sex with someone and not even know it happened? Could you even do that? And if she was pregnant, how did that happen?

With the test completed, Karla was returned back to her room. She was happy and surprised to learn her parents had gone home. This made it easier for Karla to think about everything that'd taken place in the past few hours, especially with her Mom being gone.

It wasn't long after returning to her room when a knock sounded the door. Another woman poked her head into the room and asked permission to come in.

"Hi Karla, my name is Doctor Krentza. I'm a rape counselor here at the hospital. I was hoping you wouldn't mind if I talked to you for a bit. I just want to see how you're holding up and to answer any questions you may have."

Karla spent the next hour answering Doctor Krentza's questions, most of which Karla found uncomfortable and sometimes personal. She was glad when it was over, and the doctor left her in peace.

The next visitors to enter Karla's room arrived a few hours after breakfast was served. Officer Theresa and Officer James came to ask her a few questions about what'd happened to her last night.

"Karla, are you sure you don't remember anything about last night," Officer Theresa asked.

"No, I don't," Karla replied.

"Well it is okay. The department wants to go ahead anyway with pressing charges against Gerry. We've more than enough evidence to prove he was the one, and you won't need to take the stand," Officer James told Karla.

"But I'll have to show up in court, and my parents will know," Karla argued. She feared her mom knowing about the incident most of all.

"We promise we won't say a word about this to your parents," Officer Theresa promised. "But pressing charges against Gerry is the only way to stop him from doing this to someone else."

"But there isn't enough evidence to press charges against the other guys," Officer

James said.

"What other guys," Karla asked. She couldn't remember anyone, the doctor never mentioned there was more than one guy who could've had done this to her.

"Don't you worry about that part; Carol told us everything we needed to know," Officer Theresa said.

That was the first time Karla had given any thought about her friendship to Carol. She wondered how Carol had been able to let any of this happen to her. She was supposed to be her friend. Why didn't she have her back?

Karla continued to think about Carol for the next few hours after the officers left the hospital. She wondered where Carol had been while all this was taking place. She so missed Sarah and Jody. And most of all, she really missed Jan. She could really use someone to talk to right now, someone who'd listen to her and understand.

As Officer James and Officer Theresa walked away they argued over the way the case was being handled.

"You shouldn't have told her that. Her parents have to know about any statements she makes," Officer James growled as they stepped into the elevator.

The door closed before Theresa answered, "But her Dad does know. He was told when she was brought in."

"He was told she was a victim of a drug overdose, possibly being a date rape drug, but not a definite rape victim."

"I'm sure he does know. The doctor must've told him."

"And, we don't really have enough evidence against Gerry to take this to court."

"I was fishing for more evidence. I know we don't have enough yet to convict or arrest him."

"Maybe we should forget the rape charge and go after him for his DUI, and I hear one of his passengers isn't doing well. They may not make it."

"Then we should check into it and as you say, forget the rape charge."

"At least with the DUI charge I know it'll stick."

\*\*\*

Karla was released from the hospital by noon time. Her dad arrived to take her home, saying her mom was waiting at home.

Karla's mom greeted her at the door when they arrived home, but Karla didn't stay around for long. She went almost immediately to her bedroom and found her phone. It took a few rings before Jan finally answered.

In one long breath, Karla told Jan about everything that'd happened to her since she moved.

Jan was all ears for the most part. But the last thing she asked before they ended their conversation was, "What're you going to do? Are you going to go to school on Monday?"

"Of course I'm going to school on Monday. For one thing, I'm sure Mom is going to make me even if I don't want to, and the other thing is I can't let these kids get to me. The sooner I face them the better."

"That's my sport." Jan sighed, "Well if you've any more problems and you can't get a hold of me leave me a text message. I'll get in touch with you as soon as I can."

After Karla hung up, she thought, tomorrow is another day. When she got to school tomorrow she'd give Carol one chance to come up with her version of what happened at the party. Then Karla would decide for herself whether or not Carol was worth having as a friend.

\*\*\*

Saturday was a wasted day, in more ways than one. Carol nursed her bottle for as long as she could before the effects from the liquor overcame her. She passed up on lunch and dinner without much of a fuss from her parents. They were used to this. Family-stuff just never really mattered much to her folks, for as long as Carol could remember.

Her mom and dad were always too busy relaxing on the weekends. They always claimed to have had a long or hard week at work. It was always one excuse or another, but Carol had gotten used to it. Sometimes she even thought that this was the way it was supposed to be with a family. But then she'd seen Karla's mom.

Karla's mom was the mom Carol had always wished her mom to be. The way Mrs. Centon had cared about where Karla was going, and what she was doing made Carol feel envious of her. If only her parents had cared about her as much as the Centon's cared about Karla. Maybe, just maybe Carol would've felt happier and better about herself.

Even though she'd a lot of friends, sometimes Carol felt alone. Family or no family, Carol may have just signed her own death warrant. She was sure the guys would get even with her when they found out; she was the one who'd told on them.

But maybe it wouldn't even matter. Maybe they'd never even know. She'd just have to pretend like nothing was wrong, then no one would ever know.

Why did Heath have to get involved in the first place? She wondered, what the hell was he thinking? It was supposed to be just him and her. How could he do this to her? The funny thing was, deep down inside her, she still loved him.

7 o' clock rolled around. Carol knew her dad was not a stickler when it came to grounding her, and her mom didn't even know what'd happened the other night. She was sober enough and confident enough to leave her room now. Maybe head over to Darcy's. Maybe she'd even crash over there. Darcy's mom never minded.

Carol slipped from her bedroom, through the living room where her parents were sound asleep. This was the same thing every weekend. They probably wouldn't even notice she'd left. With her bedroom door closed, they probably would never even check to see if she were still there.

Quietly, very quietly, Carol slipped out the front door and out into the street. She clutched a pint of liquor in her hoodie pocket. It was out of sight and out of mind. Just a little something if she needed it, to help her sleep.

Darcy lived in a run down, three story apartment building, up on the top floor. It was normal to hear babies crying or adults arguing in any of the apartments. Like was the case for Carol, as she made her way up the stairs to the top level.

Old drab indoor/outdoor carpet covered the floor in each hallway. The stairway was in dire need of a paint job, with several steps needing to be replaced soon. The building did have a maintenance manager, but he was not around much. The owner didn't feel the building was worth the money in repairs.

Carol was almost out of breath when she reached the top level. She should've climbed the steps slower, but she was anxious to talk to Darcy. She should know what was going on by now.

After a couple of swift raps on the door, Darcy answered, and opened the door wide to let Carol inside.

"Darren was here earlier," Darcy said while leading Carol to her room. "Said Heath, Gerry, Justin, Kyle and Mitch were in a bad accident last night. He said it was bad, real bad. Gerry was driving."

Carol took a seat by the bedroom window in the only chair in the room, a wooden chair. She slouched back against the back of the chair and rested her legs on the edge of the bed.

Darcy carried on after sitting down on the edge of her bed. "Justin may not make it. He went through the windshield. He's in a coma. I don't know about the others except that they're in bad shape."

Carol interrupted. "You don't know about Heath?"

"Darren said he'd a broken leg. He'll probably be home by tomorrow." Darcy lit a cigarette, took a drag and handed it over to Carol.

The cigarette helped Carol's nerves a bit. What she really needed was a joint or some snuff. The Captain she carried in her hoodie pocket would've to do for now.

Carol shared her pint with Darcy, and it was not long before the two of them began to feel the sleepy effects of the liquor.

She didn't know if it was the sound of the capped bottle falling out of her hand and on to the floor or if it was something else like a gunshot. Carol woke with a start. She could see Darcy all snug in her bed with her blankets drawn over herself.

Carol gritted her teeth, the back of the wooden chair digging into her spine. It hurt, and the fact she was kind of cold sitting in the chair with no blanket to cover her. She snorted to herself indignantly, thinking of how Darcy could've out of the kindness of her heart, given Carol one, just one of those many blankets she used on her bed.

She could just reach over and snatch up one of those blankets and Darcy would never notice, but why bother. Carol's back hurt from the rungs of the chair. She picked up her fallen bottle, now half empty and returned it to her hoodie pocket. Thoughts of Heath returned to her mind. At least she knew he was going to be all right. A broken leg was not all that bad, but she still was guilty for smacking him. She feared he'd never talk to her ever again.

Enough of this, Carol thought. She needed to sleep in her own bed. It was time to her to leave. This was not the first time she'd left Darcy's in the middle of the night. But first she needed to see if Darcy had any money she could borrow, to buy herself another bottle of liquor. She was sure Darcy wouldn't mind, since she did share her now almost empty pint with her.

The room was not to dark. Light flowed into the room from the streetlight outside Darcy's bedroom window. Carol could make out Darcy's purse sitting on the floor by her bureau. She quietly helped herself to the contents inside and quickly found the cash inside the wallet.

Carol was sure Darcy wouldn't miss a couple of twenties. It'd only be for a couple of days, and Darcy seemed to have over a hundred inside the billfold of her wallet.

After quietly replacing the wallet inside the purse, Carol let herself out of the bedroom. She was careful not to make a sound on her way out of the apartment. It'd be another four hours before any of the occupants would notice she was gone.

The apartment building was now quiet. There was not one sound heard as she made her way down the stairway, out the door, and onto the street. Carol knew it'd to be close to 2 in the morning. She heard the distant sound of an ankle biter barking somewhere in the neighborhood.

Now that she was totally awake and sober with a couple of bucks in her pocket, Carol decided to take a short stroll over to the mini mart on Main Street. It was not far and didn't take her long to get there. She could make out the shadow of a figure standing next to the old phone booth which was slated to be torn down by the phone company in the coming weeks.

This was where Jay could be found selling his stuff. Stuff Carol needed. Her stash at home was almost gone, and she couldn't face going without any after all that's happened this weekend.

"Hey, I need another bag." Carol told the shadow figure.

"No. You pay me for what you already have. No more credit." He told her.

"But I've to have some," she pleaded.

"You give me the sixty you owe and then I'll fix you up."

"I've forty."

Carol showed the bills to him. Jay snatched them out of her grip and told her she now owed him twenty.

"You're a ...." Carol carried on. "I need more stuff. Come on man. Please, just this one last time."

Reluctantly Jay pulled a small baggie from his pocket. "This is the last time, and the price is going up. I'm going to have to start charging you interest, so you'd better pay in within the next two days or I'll have to charge you double."

"That's robbery. You know I can't get that kind of money."

"Well you'd better figure it out, or you won't get any more stash."

Carol was pissed as she walked away, heading home. She wanted so bad to punch the guy out, but you don't beat on your dealer or he won't deal to you anymore. This meant she'd need to do some car hopping at the mall.

\*\*\*

"I friggin' hate that Bitch." Maggie said.

"Hate who?" Ashley asked while she doodled on the pad of paper.

"That new girl, Karla," Maggie hissed.

"Oh her; I guess, I don't know…I really don't have any problem with her."

"That's because she's not after your man."

"Since when was Gerry your man," Ashley asked.

"We started seeing each other two weeks ago; right up until that Bitch showed up." Maggie paused, "I know he still likes me. I just have to get rid of the Bitch before she can sink her claws into him."

"Maggie, she doesn't seem to be like that."

"I couldn't tell last night. She was all about him at the party."

"You went to the party? I heard that went over well."

"Oh yeah, it went great." Maggie said sarcastically. "I left almost as soon as it started."

"Why?"

"You think I wanted to stay around while that Bitch got to hang on my man's arm. I don't think so. And Carol, she's another frigging Bitch; she encouraged it."

"So you left before the pigs showed up?"

"Pigs … I didn't hear anything about them showing up."

"So you just left… where did you go? You should've called me."

"I came right home. I wasn't in any mood to talk to anyone." Maggie picked up her brush off her bureau and began brushing her long brown hair which fell to the middle of her back. "But I did get even." She confessed.

Ashley could only imagine what crazy Maggie had done. "I've to ask…What did you do to her?"

Maggie smirked, "I slipped a Roofie in her drink."

"Oh my God, you didn't." Ashley giggled. "And no one saw you?"

"Hell no… Gerry was too busy making goggle eyes at her, so I slipped it in her hard lemonade when he wasn't looking. Then I left."

"Oh my God… I heard she was rushed to the hospital for an Over Dose... God, Maggie, you could've killed her."

"Too bad I didn't…now I'll have to find another way to get rid of her and get my man back. By the way, I'm going to leave in a bit, heading over to the hospital to see if he's doing any better. I want to be there for him when he wakes up."

Ashley took her cue. She stood up and snatched up her sweatshirt and slipped it over the crook of her arm. It was too hot to wear it. "I've to get home now anyway. See you in school tomorrow."

Maggie followed Ashley out the front door of her townhouse apartment. "Oh if you see that Bitch, Carol – tell her I've words for her."

Ashley wave signaling acknowledgement and walked off in the opposite direction. She was glad to be on her way. Maggie was tolerable at times and then other times she was out right crazy and more than just a little bit too obsessive for her. She wondered if Gerry ever noticed Maggie was stalking him.

# AFTERWORD

Date rape happens more than people realize. It most likely will not happen the way it happened to Karla, but it still does happen. Normally the assailant is someone the victim knows and trusts.

Below is a short list of commonly used date rape drugs that have become the rave at dance clubs. They are also known as club drugs and are used for more than just date rape. Some of these drugs are used as recreational drugs by teens and young adults.

Overdoses do and can happen, and they can be accidental. These drugs like all drugs are dangerous. Their side effects alone can cause serious damage to the internal organs, like the liver and kidneys, not to mention the heart. Mixed with other substances and they can become very deadly.

# ECSTASY:

This can be known on the street by many different names ranging from X, XTC, E, Beans, the hug drug and Adam.

Ecstasy is found in pill or powder form and is used by users looking to exploit its effects that include feelings of euphoria and enhanced energy. It acts as both a stimulant and psychedelic, and is commonly used at concerts, clubs, and all-night dance parties called "raves".

Ecstasy users do face several adverse consequences, which include cognitive, physical, and psychological effects.

If taken in high doses, it can impair the body's temperature regulation, which causes increased body temperature, this can result in kidney, liver, and cardiovascular failure, and even worst cases, death. Short-term effects are like those of other stimulants, such as increased heart rate and blood pressure, involuntary teeth clenching, nausea, chills, and blurred vision. The adverse psychological effects can cause depression, sleep disruption, and anxiety. Additional risks are found, when ingesting additional chemicals that may have been added to its mix and sold as MDMA. These chemicals can include stimulants such as Ephedra, caffeine, methamphetamine, and Ketamine. Adding this just the chemical MDMA alone is hazardous. If users mix this alcohol and marijuana, they face further risk.

# GAMMA HYDROXYBUTYRIC ACID:

This is also known as Liquid Ecstasy, Liquid X, GHB, Georgia Home Boy, Easy Lay, and G.

GHB has become very popular among teens in the past few years. It has been known to be among one of the common date rape drugs. Originally used only to treat narcolepsy, this drug has found its way on to the streets. It is gaining its popularity at dance clubs and "raves".

In its common form, which is liquid, it is colorless and has a mild salty taste.

High doses of this substance can cause an overdose resulting in unconsciousness, seizures, slowed heart rate, severe respiratory depression, decreased body temperature, vomiting, nausea, coma or death. It can also inhibit the gag reflex causing the person to choke and die on their vomit.

Sustained usage can lead to addiction.

Currently there is no antidote for an overdose. The most common cause of death with this drug is respiratory arrest. Mixing this drug with alcohol or other drugs can increase the chances of this happening in the individual.

According to the US Department of Justice – Drug Enforcement Administration, it is a chemical of concern.

# ROHYPNOL:

Street name consist of Rophy, Ruffles, Roofies, Ruffies, Ruff Up, Rib, Roach 2, R2, R2-Do-U, Roche, Rope, Ropies, Circles, Circes, Forget It, Forget-Me-pill, Mexican Valium

This is a sedative that is only prescribed in Europe and Mexico as a sleep aid and anesthetic. It has the same effect to Valium, but is 10 times stronger.

With use, the user can feel sedated, intoxicated, relaxed and uninhibited for up to as much as 12 hours. This drug is sometimes used in conjunction with heroin, marijuana, or alcohol to increase the sedation. It is often taken in pill form, but to get a quick high, sometimes it is snorted or injected.

The use of Rohypnol can make the users unconscious and can cause amnesia. This makes them unable to remember what happened while they were using this chemical. Sexual assaults are commonly committed while the user is under its effects.

The company which makes Rohypnol added a blue dye to the tablets to create better detection when dissolved in drinks, but if put in blue drinks, the tablet is undetected.

Rohypnol can lower blood pressure and relax muscles. It may even nausea, dizziness, headaches, confusion, problems with the gastrointestinal system, and even problems with motor skills. All of these effects are increased if combined with alcohol or any other drugs.

Overdose results in respiratory depression, coma, and death. This normally happens when this drug is taken with alcohol.

A very addictive drug, sudden withdrawal of Rohypnol can lead to anxiety, insomnia, seizures, and psychosis.

More information on this substance can be found on the site.

Notes

(3,4-METHYLENEDIOXYMETHAMPHETAMINE (Street Names: MDMA, Ecstasy, XTC, E, X, Beans, Adams) n.d.)

(GAMMA HYDROXYBUTYRIC ACID n.d.)

(Drug Fact Sheet Rohypnol n.d.)

# Bibliography

n.d. "3,4-METHYLENEDIOXYMETHAMPHETAMINE (Street Names: MDMA, Ecstasy, XTC, E, X, Beans, Adams)." *Drug Enforcement Administration.* Accessed 2017. https://www.deadiversion.usdoj.gov.

n.d. "Drug Fact Sheet Rohypnol." *Drug Enforcement Administration Special Agent.* Accessed 2017. https://www.dea.gov.

n.d. "GAMMA HYDROXYBUTYRIC ACID." *Drug Enforcement Administration.* Accessed 2017. https://www.deadiversion.usdoj.gov.

# ABOUT THE AUTHOR

Linda Nelson attends Franklin Pierce University working on her Business degree. She lives in Southern New Hampshire, where she enjoys reading, writing, gardening, and crafting. The rest of her time she spends with her family which includes her dog and cat too.

When she wrote What Karla Wants, her son began his journey to recovery. He is still a recovering addict which prompted her to create the trilogy Wings from Ashes. Linda is a member of the Romance Writers of America (RWA) and is the author of Along Came Neil, a Young Adult Sweet-romance which is the last book in her Wings from Ashes trilogy released in 2013. To learn more about Linda or to discover up and coming events and publishing news visit her website lindajnelson.com.

Visit lindajnelson.com to learn more about upcoming releases

Carol's guilt is eating her up inside and wants to fix their friendship. She insists upon making amends by apologizing to Karla's mom but instead, the woman chases her out of the house, which is when she discovers Karla's home life isn't much different from her own. However, she still feels responsible for what happened to Karla at the party. She suggests they take a road trip with two boys they just met in hopes that their new comradeship is growing, but this only makes matters worse for the two of them when they find themselves arrested for car theft. Will Karla forgive her this time?

# ALONG CAME NEIL

There's a new boy in town, and Ashley wants him badly. Will Karla steal her man too?

Karla Centon no longer is the newest student at Brantwood High. Since moving to Brantwood six months ago, her life had been going nowhere in the right direction until she meets Neil Allard, a handsome cheerful boy who wrestles his way into her heart. Karla takes an instant disliking to Neil because she thinks he's not her type. However, what is her type? Is it tall skinny guys who wear baseball hats backwards and who happen to be bad boys or warm loveable funny guys who are more than just nice occasionally, like Neil?

Ashley likes Neil too, and her friend Maggie tries her best to keep Karla away from him. However, when Ashley starts making a big deal out of his wandering eyes, Neil doesn't like it. Karla is his friend, which is more than either of the other two girls can say. Karla begins to notice that Neil is actually rather incredible at heart. He may not have the body type she is attracted to, but his good-hearted nature attracts her instead. Finally, when Ashley throws one last tantrum at the dance over Karla, Neil has had enough. Who will really win Neil's heart?